T… …ELD

Of

Lough Gur

Michael Quinlan

Published by Lough Gur & District Historical Society.

In conjunction with Lough Gur Development Co-operative Society Ltd.

and Ballyhoura Development Ltd.

Photo of replica of Lough Gur Bronze Shield courtesy of Shannon Heritage.

Cover Design - Ross Curtin.

NDP NATIONAL DEVELOPMENT PLAN

Ballyhoura Country

Dedicated to the memory of a great friend of mine and of Lough Gur
Tom Mc Namara (1926 - 2001)

PROLOGUE.

When he heard of the muster of warriors on Aney Hill he was concerned, concerned enough to move the families with their goods and animals to the safety of Knockadoon. Garvok sensed that Nefa Rua's violence would be directed only at him. He knew this without understanding why and it made him very sad. With just six warriors he had set about defending the higher fort. This unequal struggle would not last long. Carraig Aille is easily defended but the fury of the onslaught would prevail. The two stone forts, formidable to attackers, stand on a hill, which borders Lough Gur on the eastern side. After five days of siege he alone remained. The bodies of his warriors lay scattered at various points. The stench of decayed flesh carried a message of fear.

He had killed today. The young head dangled by his side as he walked towards the remains of the house. The lighted arrows had done their job well, water being too scarce to attempt to quench the flame before it took hold. He hung the head from the charred rafter end.

"You fought well, brave young man," he conceded, and remembering the last moments and the fierce determination as the young warrior leaped over the palisade as his companions pounded the entrance gates. He knew that he was the lucky one to be alive - but for how long?

One spoil she must not have - the ancient shield!

That could only be taken if he were dead. His guardianship was a continuation that spanned more generations than anybody could tell now. In truth, he feared for the shield more than for himself and assessing the circumstances he knew that the time was approaching when it would have to be offered.

“Do the spirits want the Sun Shield?” he asked the grotesque hanging head.
In his mind he heard the answer “yes!” and he believed that the time had come to give the treasure to the spirits of the lake. Then the spirits would be on his side. He knew what he would do. Under cover of darkness, with the spirits of the night to protect him, he would go out without fear because of the mission he would be on.

The sheer precipitous west face was always free from attack. This would be his route. Before the moon rose, he took the shield from the stone-box where it was stored underground, handling it with great respect and care and with full conviction that he was doing the correct thing. Surefooted as a goat, he had no difficulty with the descent, nor in finding the boat hidden in the reeds. He placed the shield in the boat and climbed in himself and pushed out from the shore.

A tall man stood up in the small boat and held a magnificent, perfectly-made bronze shield above his head. He spoke the words of offering in his mind and they roared within him. He lowered his hands and from waist-high and with all his strength he cast the disc from him. It skimmed through the air, low at first, then rising. A sudden break in the cloud and the moon struck it and it shone like a streak of lightning as it dipped and entered the water, still shining as it cut a path to the bottom. A wolf howled at the moon.

Years grew to centuries and the progress of the seasons brought growth and decay on land and in the water. Nobody ever returned to seek out the ancient shield. Nobody knew where it lay. It sometimes sheltered fish. Creatures of the mud often surfaced under it and despaired at their imprisonment. Before many autumns had passed, a light covering of silt hid it. It took longer for its leather lining to decay and disappear. An object so beautiful and prestigious should hardly have been allowed to moulder there. What of the spirits? Anyway there it stayed. Above it many changes took place, the biggest during a time when a terrible starvation caused death throughout the land. To drain the lake, or partly so, was a scheme devised to create work so that money might be earned to buy food. There was much reluctance. The 'curse of the Fitzgeralds' was greatly feared. Who would be brave enough to disturb the underwater kingdom of Gearóid Iarla deep in the lake of Lough Gur? Eventually hunger and certain death prevailed on many to work and the cries of famished children and mothers proved the stronger. A channel was dug from the northwest corner of the lake and even when it cut through the graveyard and bones bespoke the reality of death and disturbance of the generations past, the work continued to completion.

It was considered remarkable how many objects of bronze and stone were found when the new lower shoreline was established. Collecting and selling these artefacts of the ancient peoples put food on tables and paid passage to other countries where prospects seemed brighter. Famous people came to see and left wondering at what they had seen. Learned men attached many explanations and they came from lands far away and most often didn't return home empty-handed. The small lake became marsh and semi-bog and as it dried out rushes and reed spread across it from the shore. In summer it was possible to cross to the hill and one had only to avoid the few deep holes that remained. Somewhere within, the ancient shield remained hidden.

It was the early autumn of 1872. The summer had been exceptionally warm and dry, which allowed for quick progress with hay saving. With winter fodder secure there was some time to spare and this time could be put to use to earn some little money. Good reed for thatching was always in demand and the best reed was out towards the middle of what was once part of the lake, easily accessible to young lads with light step. That's where Cahal, now twenty-two, and his young brother, Séamus, aged fifteen, had spent the morning. Cahal was cutting with the sickle and Séamus was binding. The sun beat down and there was no shelter. Their browned, shirtless bodies glistened with sweat. As the sheaves of reed grew, Cahal often glanced admiringly at his brother who worked at a pace that belied his youth. Admiration was mutual between the brothers.

Shortly after midday they stopped and rested, lying flat on their backs, eyes closed against the sun. They heard the sound of children at play in the water beyond. A skylark's song forced them to squint at the blue sky. The insects were troublesome and needed constant removal. A loud splash in the pool nearby told of fish presence in the remaining pools. The sound reminded Cahal of the bottle of milk submerged in the pool, suspended in the cool water. That and the slices of bread were their food and drink. He roused himself.

"Will we eat or jump?" he asked his brother.

Without saying a word, Séamus got up and ran back along the path and crouched in a starting position. Cahal drew a line in the ground with the sickle.

“You jump from here,” he called, “ and I will mark where you land. If I can’t jump that much farther than you (he stretched out his hands) then you will win. You can have three jumps.”

Séamus rushed forward and sailed through the air.

“I’ll have trouble beating this,” Cahal thought as he drew the point of the sickle through the peaty ground where Séamus’ heels had landed.

“That’s good!” he said, “try again.”
The point of the sickle had stuck in something and he thought that it sounded metallic, but he pulled it free and watched his brother preparing to jump again.

It was fortunate that Séamus landed a few inches forward rather than behind, because had he not, the shield might never have been found. This time the metallic sound was clear and the point was harder to remove.

“Séamus, we’ve found something,” Cahal said and his heart began to race with an excitement sprung from knowing that many had been well rewarded for a good find. Séamus was on his knees beside him now and they began peeling the turf away and as they did so they saw and recognised the shield for what it was. Through the dirt they saw the rings and the bosses and the two sickle holes and Cahal knew he had something valuable.

Séamus wasn’t impressed.
“It’s only an auld bit of tin,” he ventured but he saw the excitement in Cahal’s eyes and it struck him with awful force that he could lose his brother to the land across the sea.

He knew he wished to go there and was saving towards it. A great sadness came on him.
"Leave it there. Throw it away," he exclaimed as the tears welled in his eyes.
Cahal held the soiled, wounded, lustreless shield out from him and he thought the sun caught it in one spot.

"This is my passage to America. And yours," he added after a brief pause.
A strange sound was heard from the old fort above and brought a chill of fear.

CHAPTER ONE

Often she had wished that her responsibilities were not so demanding, that she could indulge her personal whims without being the focus of the attention of all. Had they forgotten that she was a warm and passionate woman who had become emotionally drained directing other people's lives? As she dwelt on these matters she knew that she was not being fair, either to herself or the people who depended so much on her. She fought to banish these thoughts, which she knew were caused only by the events of the day. Three things combined to bring her back to reality. The first was the chill breeze of evening that sprang up from the lake; its sting chided her and brought a shiver to her spine.

"Someone else walking over my grave," she thought, and that did not help.

The laughter of children was the second help. This was a reason for not giving into the pressure. She recognised the voices of some of her own among them and she raised her head a little higher. The third was the bell that sounded from the monastery on the lakeshore. The monastery stood directly below the fort on the sheltered side and depended on the occupants of the fort for protection. For this they paid in prayer and in the teaching of some of the youth. As far as Nanda was concerned the best benefit was the good advice she always got from the ageing abbot, Becan, who was father to her second son. It wasn't just advice. It was a deep and much-needed friendship, which she had decided to copper-fasten ten years before when Becan was stronger than now. At her insistence they had agreed to procreate together. She convinced him that it should be because of the strong qualities they carried between them and which she hoped could be transferred to a son or daughter. It was a time of gender equality. She recalled Becan's initial reluctance but her firm insistence was linked to a guarantee of continued protection. She had kept her promise that theirs would be one encounter and only one. She had feigned illness and sent for Becan to console her with prayer, had asked that her other children and servants be taken elsewhere to sleep and thus had she and Becan spent the night together. The memory was forever. The boy, Garvok, was the living proof. When she was sure that her conception dates had passed, she took one of the menfolk of the fort to her bed each night, as was her entitlement, for several nights. Only the wisest knew of Garvok's origins.

Look at her! She is magnificent! She stands akimbo between the forts looking down on the lake. Her shock of red-gold hair is being caught by the wind. Her face is perfectly formed with high forehead and blue eye, slightly arched nose over full lips over strong chin. When she smiles, as she is doing now, her teeth are clean. Her body is tall and well-formed, full-breasted and nimble, not showing signs of the children she has borne, her hips and legs make strong contact with the ground. She is well-dressed and that gold neck-ornament and bracelets imply authority.

Why is she smiling? She has just cast off the lethargy that was upon her. She turns towards the monastery and moves to the less steep side of the hill. She knows that Becan will be there.

She rarely enters the monastery other than for Mass, which she attends only irregularly. Becan has been informed of her approach and has come out to meet her. This is a regular occurrence and their walk by the lakeshore is always vacated when they set out. They do not exchange greetings other than a nod of acknowledgement. The sun will set within the hour. They will be back before it does. Two swans are close to the shore with their five grey cygnets, feeding.

"That's how we should be," she taunted.
His wistful traces of a smile and light of eye give assent but the words do not.
"Do you not have troubles enough, woman?"
"Today I have plenty but I hope for a different morrow," was her reply.

There were people on top of the high hill and the animals were grazing the slope even in the most precarious places. They were being gathered in for the night. The barking of the dogs echoed across the water. They were walking fairly quickly and she became conscious of a drag in his breathing and slowed the pace.

"Today I lost ten cattle and two of my men were killed. I am honour bound to seek revenge but I am not sure that I have the strength to do so, but I must try, and try I will."

He knew that she would, she had to. He knew she hadn't come to him to be advised not to. He knew the rules as well. He knew she needed to speak and that she spoke in the hope that he could help and give her courage to do what at times seemed almost impossible.

"Woman, your pride will be your undoing, and of your people and of my monks and monastery. You are no longer strong enough to fight this persistent enemy without help and you continue to refuse to seek help from your kinsfolk, and in particular from your brother,"

She almost snorted her angry reply. He had heard it many times before.
"Never! Never!" and even though her eyes flared in anger, Becan knew that the resolve was weakening as her warrior number decreased.

"Nanda, you are running out of choices. I know that no matter what difficulties there may have been between your brother and you, he will still come to your aid. Times are changing. Men are in control of many tribes again. You know the burden of leadership and look to the day when Garvok will take that burden from you. Be sure you have something to give him, otherwise you will have betrayed your trust."

His words fell softly on her ear and she knew that what he said was true, would come to pass. She shrugged her shoulders, tossed her proud head and walked away from him. She stopped just as quickly.
"He will never get the Sun Shield".

Becan knew that he was making an impact.
"He will never get the Sun Shield," and she spoke with very positive force but Becan knew that it would not be long before he would be visiting Garaun. He also knew that he would not fail.

The sun dipped behind the high hill. They had enough discussion for one evening. At the monastery gate they parted with a friendly nod and smile; both happy for each other's company and for the decision almost taken. She didn't even react to the barking dog as she entered the fort. A weary sentry reprimanded him and wished her a good night. Night brought peace!

CHAPTER TWO.

Carraig Aille is a defensive contradiction on the one hand, and yet very well chosen and sited on the other. Militarily, the island-hill of Knockadoon is a natural fortress which makes the presence of such a great stone fortress so close by seem a little strange but violent times demand unusual measures. It was as a result of violence that Carraig Aille came to be. It was built strangely enough to protect the island-hill by presenting itself as a focus for attack into which the people gathered hastily with limited material belongings when attack was imminent. They didn't always manage to get there on time and the toll was often high. The late approach from Knockadoon was by boat across the small lake and a clamber up the western cliff that often proved impossible for the old.

Garvok was unusually curious for one so young.
"I know where that comes from," Nanda thought to herself.
To him she explained, "It was a time of trouble, not unlike the present. The island-hill was often attacked and many of our young people taken into bondage; the old were generally killed. That still happens, as you know. It was decided to build a strong fort here in which people could shelter in time of attack."
"There are two now," Garvok interrupted.
"In the beginning there was only one and it was like that for a long time, but in another time of trouble and unexpected attack and death, when many of our warriors were killed, it was decided to build this fort for protection and as a dwelling place."
She pointed to the fort on the hilltop, which was now the home of the warriors, the few who survived.
"That became the home of the soldiers."

Some of Garvok's friends had come quietly towards the two in conversation and when they were noticed it was a signal for Garvok to go and play. Without a word he touched his mother's arm gently, smiled and ran happily away.
"Stay young as long as you can," she whispered, "great is the task ahead".

This feeling of being alone, even though there were people about, was disturbing. It was at such moments that Becan came to the rescue with his quiet talk and sound advice. There was also something else that soothed and reinforced responsibilities, that was looking at the Sun Shield, the ceremonial shield that carried more tribal status than all their possessions put together. She went inside her house and removed the skins, which covered the stone box in which it was kept. It had been kept there for hundreds of years. Hundreds, yes, but nobody knew how many. It had been a tribal possession since the legendary smith, Dicol, whose ancestors had brought metal and horses from across the seas, cast it.

The covering stone was heavy, and it always brought the tombs to mind. That she did not particularly like. She was well strong enough to remove it but one of her bondswomen was just then tending to the fire and she called to her for assistance. Together they lifted it up on one side and tipped it to lie flat beside the opened box. Nanda nodded to have the next coverings removed. This moment was always special - the moment of unveiling. It was always thrilling and she watched as she knelt and the kneeling was a reverence. Even in the darkness of the stone box it seemed to glow when exposed and this moment of intensity was a prelude to the ever-sacred handling, this raising-up as from the tomb, a symbol of continuance and ancestral support. The bondswoman, realising the intensity of the moment, sat back on her heels and covered her face with her arms. She shivered in fear and Nanda didn't reassure her because she was no longer conscious of her presence. Holding the shield with both hands at arms length she walked from the house.

As she walked towards the rampart the work of the evening stopped. The women wiped their hands on their skirts and pots near the boil were removed from above the flames. The girls milking the cows also stopped work and wiped hands likewise. The smith cooled the piece of iron in the tank of water and the loud hiss was louder in the silence, which had descended. Whenever the Sun Shield was brought out this was the procedure.

"Pagan practices!" Becan scoffed. "You lead your people backwards rather than forward."
She knew he wasn't serious. Well, not really serious, since he had grown up to be aware of the wisdom in acknowledging the many differing spirits that controlled the destiny of life.

"Go back to your church and books and bells," she would reply, "I will place my trust in the old spirits. I will send signals of my troubles to the spirits of land and sky and water and they will answer me. You can talk to your one god, I to my many."
There was no problem between them and Becan had even come to gaze on the shield on a few occasions. That was a real sign of friendship.

At the entrance gates two youths stood. They had anxiously awaited this moment. They had known for some time that it was their turn to hold the shield aloft until sunset. They had practised holding objects high up for as long as possible, to strengthen their arms. To fail to keep the shield aloft would be a great indignity to the shield and its spirits, to family and to themselves. The ridicule would be hard to bear.

Nanda now raised the Sun Shield and held it towards her. It caught the rays of the dipping sun and turned to flame. For a moment she became transformed, as the blazing shield became her head. The sheer majesty of the moment brought exclamations of wonder though all had seen many times. The youths stood on the rise directly outside the entrance and as Nanda approached, they took the shield. They became the holders of ancient power. So as to extend the magnificence a section of palisade was removed so that the sun could be reflected until it dipped behind Ardaghlooda, by which time the youths would be exhausted in body but elevated in mind. They would also be rewarded in that they were now accepted as being well on the road to manhood.

No wonder Becan was critical! From his Christian viewpoint, this was akin to idolatry. In actual fact it was a mixture of the old and new and the shield certainly belonged to the old. It contained a great knowledge of the movements of the sun and moon which were long forgotten and which nobody could interpret anymore. The people were on their knees and they were praying, sometimes Christian prayers and other times ancient sounds and incantations often meaningless to the speakers but important in tradition. They knew of the Christ but they hadn't seen him. They admired Becan and his monks, admired their way of life, believed what they told them and tried to live in the fashion asked but this was very difficult. The sun god asked nothing but whispered codes of good behaviour through the spirits. Now and then the spirits needed offerings but not very often. The monks were much more demanding. The sun god came to them and was with them as now and while he was with them it was a time to ask for the necessities of life from he who gave them. The more one asked the more one got. He came among them in the Sun Shield when he prompted Nanda to bring it forth but he was often among them in the sparkling lake water and in the decorative objects that were worn with great pride. Hardly a day passed when he didn't come close.

Though time seemed to stand still for the entranced beholders, its passage wasn't checked and now it seemed that the shield was reflected in the sky as it blazed in sunset. The lower edge of the shield was touched by the shadow of the rampart and as the sun went lower the shadow rose. The curtain was spreading rising from bottom to top; the glory was slowly ending. Not so slowly now as the top half was reached and time passing became real. Moments of controlled frenzy found expression in gasps and sighs, in shouts of ecstasy and cries of despair. The one were already assured that their wishes would be granted, the other feared that time hadn't been used to the full. The curtain was fully lifted and the shield became dark. For some moments the holders seemed frozen in time. Tired muscles rippled and young bodies now shone in their cover of perspiration. Then they lowered it and brought it into Nanda's house, as was their direction. Their family members looked on in pride.

Nanda would remain where she was until total darkness came and the stars came out. She would wait for the blessing of the moon, which would fill the sky to-night. Most of the others would stay with her and their wait would be a silent one.

A bondswoman wrapped a cloak about her shoulders. The tinkling of the monastery bell calling day's end wafted through the air and passed over unheard.

CHAPTER THREE.

Sweeter than bird-song! That was the best compliment that could be paid to Tana's lovely voice, and it was freely and often paid. It mingled with the bird-song each morning as she milked the cow in the little field in which hers and Smet's house stood. Smet hadn't heard her rising and he now awoke to her song, turned to make sure that her place was empty, hoped for a moment that it might not be, stretched, yawned and settled back to listen, for the moment insensitive to the annoying body-lice that were constantly pestering.

Were it not for the singing neither would the young cow be standing still. Lithe, lively she kicked with considerable and dangerous power. Her calf had been still-born and the old cow who had been milk supplier to the family for years had died also that spring. The young cow was the three-year-old daughter of the old and it was right that she should carry on the work. Easier said than done! Smet and two of his neighbours and kinsmen fought and struggled on nose, horns and rope while Tana attempted the milking. They were never going to succeed and all the struggling seemed in vain but then Tana began to croon softly and everything changed. This sound was as familiar to the young cow as had been her mother's lowing and equally soothing. The struggle ended and never restarted. The price was the calming song, the reward the free-flowing rich milk which nourished the family and maintained its good health.

Smet lay still listening and watching the dust-motes floating in the sunbeam that entered through the partly open door at the back of the house. Across the room the children stirred but didn't wake, their little bodies still recharging after the sapping high-summer activities of yesterday. Tana and her song filled his mind. Strange things were happening. That sweet voice was in much demand and was often and well rewarded. She had sung for and brought comfort to many the sick child and persons young and old. Most often it was sound without words but she had many songs with words also and she made her own songs and honoured occasions and great happenings with new compositions. Most recently she had been asked to attend houses visited by death and her plaintive expression of sorrow was joined in by others in dignified lamentation which very often lasted until it brought exhaustion and escape from hurt and loss. Just then the singing stopped. The milking was done. Smet rose to greet his wife at the door as she entered with her jar brimful of warm milk. They acknowledged each other with a nod and Smet smiled a gentle smile of appreciation of her beauty as he took the jar from her and drank deeply.

The children were now awake and came forward tow-headed and naked and hungry. The youngest, a boy of two and a half and only recently weaned, ran to her and when she took him in her arms he immediately sought her breast, but she gently took his hand and mouth away and put him down on the floor.

"Big boy will drink out of bowl like Tem," to which the nine-year old Tem replied, "I want to drink out of the jar like Smet."

The girl was five and named Nata. All three had been born strong and were well-developed and strong-limbed for their ages. Smet looked on silently as he wiped the milk-froth from his beard.

"Go out and relieve yourselves and then go down to the lake and wash. Tem, take the boy with you," Tana ordered. "When you come back your food and milk will be ready." Whatever reluctance there may have been quickly disappeared when Smet started towards them and made a little growl-like sound in his throat.

"It is time we named the boy."

For Tana to speak thus was a declaration that the child was healthy and would survive. Smet agreed. If health was in doubt the naming would be postponed and death often removed the need to name anyway in too many children. Knowing that she had most likely a name ready he asked what she had in mind.

"Let him be called Etan," she said simply, and from then on that was his name.

Before the children returned, Becan called. After greetings were spoken he was offered, and accepted, a bowl of milk.
"I met the children by the shore," he said, "and they are in great health. You are doing your job well." He paused before continuing.
"Tem and Nata told me that the young boy is as yet unnamed. This should not be."
Tana was quick to answer.
."His name is Etan, Becan. He has just been named a moment ago. Isn't it a good name?"

Smet was proud of her, almost convinced that she knew this encounter was to take place. But Becan was their friend and his concern was because of that friendship.

Quietly he said, "Then you should take him to the church and call down God's blessings on him, and on yourselves and the other children also."

This would not be unacceptable to either Smet or Tana but they would not have thought of doing it were it not for Becan's suggestion. They were more concerned about their own gods and their treatment of them than of the Christian god that Becan and his monks spoke so much about.

The decision would be Smet's and he readily agreed and an arrangement was made. Smet's attempt at enthusiasm was not lost on Becan but he was pleased because Smet was a person of influence in his own right as well as in being Nanda's younger brother.

"You are wiser than your sister," Becan added a little wistfully.
The noisy return of the children ended that conversation.

"Your name is Etan," Tana announced holding the little boy by the shoulders at arm's length.
"Do you like your name?"
"Etan! Etan! Etan!", the child repeated smiling and happy. The other children began chanting the name and eventually Smet, Tana and Becan joined in and they all joined hands around the little boy and the happy repetition implanted the name in everybody' mind. They finished in organised fashion with one great shout of "Etan" and then all sank down onto the floor embracing each other and laughing. Becan was first to realise that such a position was perhaps beneath his dignity and that he might be intruding on a personal family affair. He stood up and Tana was quick to recognise his embarrassment and went to him and gently held his hand and he knew that he was as much part of this

naming process as he would be in a church one and for a moment he questioned his new-found beliefs and felt the pleasure of glimpsing a youth long gone.

Two short sharp bell peals called Becan back to the monastery.

"I am needed so I had better return. Farewell!" he said. "At least it isn't the alarm call of trouble."

Smet and Tana walked outside with him. Below the lake shone in the morning sun. What a good place to be, thought Becan. This stretch of level land was halfway up Drumliagh (The Grey Ridge). It was about one hundred paces long by forty wide and was divided into four small enclosed fields. Once there was a house in each but at this time Smet's was the only house. It was in the north field and he used the four fields. The hill rose behind sheltering from the east and a rough step system led down to the water's edge and was known as the "staighree". Becan began the descent to the shore.

"Go carefully," Smet called and then added. "Wait! I need to call on Eral and will be part of the way with you."
His step was much surer than Becan's on the steep incline.

CHAPTER FOUR.

Big eels slept in the mud of the stream that is the outlet of the lake. After a short distance it disappears underground in a chorus of rumblings and gurglings. Esk knew the place well. It was his favourite fishing place and rightly so. This morning he had taken four sturdy eels. They lay, still wriggling, on the bottom of his little boat even though the fish spear had in each case severed the spinal cord. The spear was his pride and joy as well as being a regular supplier of good food as it was this morning. Smet had lovingly forged it to a design that they had worked out together and the fact of using three prongs was innovative. They hadn't seen one similar before although Smet had made others since. But a trident fishing-spear was only as good as its handler. There was a need for an instinct that told of where the eel slept. Esk was uncanny in this regard. His were the full skills of the hunter, which earned him a good living and much respect.

The sounds of the morning hadn't disturbed his work or concentration. As the sun brightened the sky over Drumliagh he saw and heard the birds begin their day as the mists were drawn up from the lake. The highpoint of the early day was Tana's singing as she milked her cow. He had already crossed the water at that stage. When the shouts and laughter of the children reached him, as they reacted to the cold sting of first contact with water, he turned and waved, knowing that they were seeing him also. Their shrill shouts echoed across the water. A little later when the light of day had flooded the lake he saw Becan move slowly along the lakeshore, heard, but didn't understand his exchange of words with the children, and then more slowly climb the steep 'staighree'.

The lake surrounded the great island, which had been home to countless generations of families since man first came to live in this area. Esk's crannog (man-made island) was offshore to the northeast of the great island, as if the great island had at some stage given birth. Esk often marvelled at the amount of work which went into its construction as the water was deep at this point and it had needed huge amounts of material to make the little island. This had been done some five generations previously. Four other crannogs had been built in the lake around the same time and three were still occupied. Esk would joke that the crannog was a much better sanctuary than the great stone forts that needed many soldiers to defend. The twisting underwater entrance causeway to the crannog had deterred many intruders and Esk had not always answered the calls for help. Second attempts were rarely made.

He heard his name being called. It was his mother's unmistakable shrill voice and when she called he responded as always. She was by far the oldest person in the community and was greatly respected and feared. People couldn't understand how she had lived so long and suspected that she was of the spirits and it was said that she would live forever. She seemed never to change. She was old when those who were now old had been young. Esk was getting old. His hair colour was changing. Pains were creeping into his bones especially in winter and his mother hadn't an ailment of any kind.

"Coming!" he shouted back and his voice echoed back across the water to him. Satisfied with his morning catch he propelled his small boat in a zigzag path across the water pulling two or sometimes three strokes on each side with his single oar. He saw plenty of activity around the monastery; work in many forms was in progress. Two sentries were in the watchtower that stood within the hillfort. Wisps of cloud were stationary and the sun made the calm water sparkle.

She was pleased when she saw the eels even if she didn't say so. Esk knew by the trace of smile on her wrinkled face.
"Your food is ready."
She ate with him and managed to chew the meat with her toothless jaws. Neither spoke until the meat and bread had all been eaten and washed down with water from the lake.

"Lots of fish?"
"Yes," he answered, "but they will leave soon and it will be time to catch many and food will be plentiful."
"Get yourself a woman. You need a woman. I will not be here much longer to care for you."

To this he did not reply. Each morning at this time she said the same thing; had been saying it for years and would continue to do so. Esk had long ago stopped answering. He went outside and sat on the bank and left his feet hang in the water. Bending down he raised handfuls of water to his face and further handfuls to wet his shaggy hair and he dreamed of what might have been.

Smet's shout roused him.
"Come! We have matters to discuss with Eral,"

Esk remembered and seeing his two friends on the lakeshore he moved to his boat and headed towards the point where Becan was also beckoning. In the world of general silence in which he lived with his mother there was no need for explanations of departures, nor arrivals for that matter, just the curt crisp calls to food, the declaration of impending death and the admonition to take a wife. Anyway, having eaten, the old woman had returned to her bed and he could hear her loud snores and thus she would remain until hunger called her again. A couple of easy strokes took him to the shore.

"Saw you at work early," was Becan's salute. "A good plump eel would be good for an ageing abbot."

Esk acknowledged with a slight incline of the head, which Becan recognised as a positive, and that he would have more than one eel before long. The boat was secured and the three proceeded along the shore.

"The boy's name is Etan," Smet told Esk proudly. Again Esk acknowledged with the nod of the head.
"I want to teach him all about fishing when he is older. I give you a responsibility for him."
And again Esk nodded. This friendship worked well with the minimum of words.
"We will celebrate in the church one day soon," Becan added.

They reached the shallow entry-point to the island-hill. Here they stopped and Becan invited them to the monastic settlement and promised refreshment. Both Smet and Esk declined and turned to go across the hill to the fort.
"God be with you both," Becan called.

"And with you," the two replied with what Becan thought was limited sincerity and they added, "Let the spirits keep good watch over you."

Smet and Esk didn't go very far before stopping at the rock well, which was always full of ice-cold water. Everybody knew that this well had special properties because it had to have been put there by the spirits. Who else could make water come out of a rock? They watched Becan move slowly towards the busy monastery. Then with cupped hands they drank the cool water and grinned appreciation at one another. The sun was moving high in the sky and the day was really warm.

"My sister needs help but she won't admit it," Smet remarked as he stood up and looked towards the fort.

"She needs the protection of Garaun but pride does not allow her to ask for it."

"I have spoken to her many times but it isn't of any use. She claims he will demand the shield and she has sworn never to yield that."

"She may well not be able to protect it if these attacks continue," Esk spoke slowly and almost sharply. Each word took an effort to make.

"Try again and take Becan to speak with Garaun. Something must be done."

Smet shrugged inferring the hopelessness of a concerned young brother whose voice didn't carry enough weight as yet.

"Come on!" he said and they set off again.

Why had the bird-song stopped? Esk's hunting instincts demanded sharp reaction. He sensed there was something wrong. The two were in the dip north of the fort. The grove of trees gave cover to the east. Smet felt a chill on his spine, he felt fear. He wished he had brought a weapon with him. Esk had his fish spear. He was never without it.

The arrow smashed into Smet's neck severing his jugular vein. The impact cast him to the ground in a scream of pain and disbelief. His blood gushed through his fingers as he tried to free the tormenting arrow. He called for Tana as a misty darkness spread over his eyes. Esk was with him now pleading, consoling, willing him to live, assuring him that he would be well, telling him to wait for Tana and the words came between tears and sobs. Smet stopped struggling, he no longer felt pain. He lay still and in his quiet he imagined he heard Tana singing her sweetest song and coming ever closer. He stretched out his hands to her, smiled, closed his eyes and lay still.

Now the only sound came from Esk. It began deep within him, the cry of a hurt beast, and it gained in volume and anger to climax in a roar of heart-rending futile fury and he held his dead friend commingling blood and tears

Smet's killer was dead. He lay at the edge of the grove. Having fired the fatal arrow he had turned to escape but Esk's fishing spear entered his back in a triple-kill. He lay prostrate with the spear handle pointing to the sky. His companion, whose arrow had missed Esk, had escaped among the trees. Esk didn't pursue.

All of these sounds reached the fort and were interpreted as being the prelude to another attack. There was much bustle to man defences and get in readiness. But no attack came and after a while Nanda sent two armed men out to investigate the dip that was hidden from the fort.

The birds had begun to sing again.

CHAPTER FIVE.

The shield was brought out again on the evening of the day of Smet's death - Smet's murder, Smet's killing. What matter? The result was the same anyway. The occasion was quite different from the previous one. There was no expectation of direction from the spirits. The message was clear to everyone. The demand was for revenge of the bloodiest and most devastating. Then why bring out the shield? To calm the frenzy and properly direct the anger and fury. The focussing was on course until a heavy cloud obliterated the setting rays.

"This is not a good sign," Nanda said in grieving tone, "but good or bad we know what must be done."

This comment was acknowledged only by the nodding of heads when one might have expected a great roar of intent. That would come later.
"Put the shield away," was her next comment and this was done much to the disappointment of the holder-youths. They had been deprived and may well have a long wait until their chance came again.

Tana's dignity had withstood the test. Her lamentation over her dead man wrung hearts and prevented anybody interrupting the process until she lay down beside the dead body, drained to exhaustion. Never had such sounds been heard. It contained all the cries previously unknown to man. It chilled on the dark side when death and loss was the clear theme, and yet it also thrilled when it echoed their love for each other and the happiness of a time together, and it wrenched when it spoke of their separation until they would be together again. The birds were silent once again but her cries and words of sorrow and love sometimes evoked howls from the dogs and cows bellowed as they struggled to understand this heaviness in the air. Esk stood watching all of this, his only movement being in the fluttering of an eyelid when the sorrow reached a point where it seemed her heart must surely break and Smet and Tana would be together again. No matter how much it may have seemed it could not be because Tana knew her duty to their children.

Becan and his monks came to give comfort but knew better than to interfere and when the personal mourning was over it was then too late because of Tana's drained state. However a monk with medical skills gave her a potion which would ensure a restful sleep for many hours. The women had taken the children to other homes. It would be some weeks before Smet's decomposed and partially cremated body would be placed on the summit of the high hill and join others in the foetal position and keep watch on those below.

Esk's old mother, the ancient who was to live forever, chose to die also on that day. Having eaten, and admonished Esk, she slept and didn't wake again. It was a strange happening. One wonders if she were aware of the events of the day and the consequences for her son? It was evening when Esk returned and found her. This death didn't affect him as much as the earlier one. The bonds of parent and child had long hardened into a tolerance, but not without love. Esk was exhausted by the happenings of the day but decisions are often more easily made at that stage. He looked on his dead mother for some minutes, his mind filled with gratitude for the years past, and there was sorrow but not much. Esk realised that she had chosen her time of death, having seen the day unfold through the window of sleep.

Her open mouth was a toothless cavity, her eyes bright and staring as if scanning her life's journey and showing surprise neither at life nor at death. Strings of dirty white hair fell sparsely from an almost hairless crown, one or two crossing the wrinkled face-space. The wrinkles continued down the neck-space but when Esk slit and removed her tunic, the body was strangely different. Her flesh was clean and white though scarce on the thin body and the breasts were no more than nipples fallen from position left and right in empty tucks of skin. Her pubic area was hairless above fleshless thighs. Hands and feet were the gnarled extremities of hardship and exposure, time-frozen contortions of work, injury and pain.

Esk took a necklace of pike vertebrae and fitted it on her. There was a plentiness of eel-skin and he put lengths about her head and on wrists, ankles and joined two pieces to surround her waist. With the remainder he stuffed the open mouth and then he lifted the body effortlessly and placed it in his boat. It filled the boat, the head resting on the prow, feet appearing above the stern. All the while he spoke to the spirits, commending her spirit to them and then he was ready to set out.

The rising wind sent ripples across the water as Esk pushed the boat and its contents across the lake towards the channel where his day had begun. There was nobody about to notice. Reaching the channel he could stand on the soft mud. His head and shoulders were still above the gunwale of the boat. He affixed stoneweights at neck, waist and ankles and then turned the boat over and the weighted body fell to the lake-bottom landing face downward. Esk went underwater to place it on its back and make sure it looked south to the morning sun. He put the legs apart to stabilise; the unweighted hands rose towards the surface. He waited until the mud settled, having righted the boat. He continued to commend her to the spirits. As the water cleared he saw again the staring eye and the floating hands and was satisfied.

The fury of the storm took him by surprise. The rain struck like a deluge. The wind caught his boat and sent it spinning through the water uncontrolled. And Esk just sat there impervious to all that was happening about him. A flash of lightning tore the sky and engulfed the lake. Thunder leaped from hill to hill and then the fury struck Esk and he stood up in the boat and roared cries of anger and sorrow. Wild, wild animal sounds overpowered the elements and he spat out words that he never knew before. He held his spear aloft and lighting came again and struck it and sent it flying form his hand, splintering one prong and landing it in the water close to his dead mother's body.

Time passed again. The night was quieter. The rain had stopped and heavy black clouds were sweeping across the wild sky. When he became conscious he was lying on the lakeshore, his boat cast up beside him. He knew where he was. He got up and climbed the staighree. The dogs barked and snarled but didn't approach. Pulling the heavy hide aside he heard the breathing within and knew that the children were back with Tana. He knew where to find her.

A male replacement child was conceived that night.

CHAPTER SIX.

The old people were wise about these things. They had seen many objects yielded up from the lake. Some had worked on the "cutting" during the hungry years. Old James Butler had, and was a friend of all the antiquaries. His advice was what Cahal needed. His father had said so when he saw the shield. He recognised that it had some value but wondered because of its seemingly poor condition and especially the two holes made by the sickle.

"Old James is your man. Take it to him and he'll tell you what to do."
"Will you come with me?" Cahal asked, but his father shook his head. There was work to be done and it was enough that one of them should go. He looked at his son, almost regretting his refusal, but wanting the lad to stand on his own two feet because he was fairly sure that the shield would part them and maybe forever. They had decided not to show the shield to his mother, as she was superstitious about things taken from the lake area, fearing the wrath of the spirits. There were tales of bad luck following what seemed to be good fortune. She would have insisted that it be shown to the priest and blessed. Cahal and his father were not free of superstition either but they felt that if the priest made an offer for the shield it could hardly be refused, and if the mother were there then it most certainly could not. The same thing applied to the landlord, the Count, but he was away at the moment anyway and would not be returning for a month or so.

"Take it to Old James. He will see you right," said the father again. "Take Séamus with you since he helped you to find it."

Séamus, who had been standing beside Cahal, tugged at his jacket to encourage departure. Cahal swung the canvas bag containing the shield across his shoulder. He had put some hay in the bag also to hide the shape of the contents. They set off.

"Go by the small lake and over the fort," their father called. "That way you will not meet curious people. You can be sure that Old James will keep your secret."

How things had changed in such a short time! Cahal wasn't free of fear that the shield would bring bad luck, nor was he free of fear of the prospect of emigrating, but the challenge and sense of adventure won through. He directed his thoughts on the positive prospect and it lightened his step and Séamus was hard-pressed to keep pace. To slow him down, Séamus called "Who do you think owned the aul' shield?"

He refused to show regard of any sort for it. He saw it as an enemy from the moment of finding, a stealer of his relationship with his brother.

"We'll ask Old James, but I'm sure it belonged to a powerful person, a king or warrior."

"And how did he lose it?"

"I don't know. Maybe he was crossing the lake in a boat and a storm struck and the shield fell into the water."

"Or maybe when the storm came, he threw the shield in the water to quieten the spirits of the storm."

Cahal stopped and looked at his young brother in surprise. This sounded strange coming from one so young but then he realised that the stories were often told of how all the objects were found in the lake and the theory of giving offerings to the spirits was the one most put forward.

"Who told you that?"

"Granny. She tells great stories about the people who lived here long ago. She talks of kings and queens and warriors with golden swords and times when everybody was happy and nobody poor. You've heard her tell them yourself many times."
He had but hadn't taken much interest, certainly not as much as his younger brother it seemed.

Breath came short and fast as they climbed to the fort and when they reached the top they sat on the wall beside the steps to rest.
"There's where we found it," said Séamus pointing down.
Cahal was feeling uneasy and didn't know why. He was sure that he was imagining things but he thought that a strange heat had come from the bag with the shield. He thought at one stage that the hay had gone on fire but by then he had just reached the fort and had thrown the bag on the ground. When he dared look inside all was the same as before. Séamus noticed his ill ease.
"What's wrong with you?" he asked.
Cahal picked up the bag and brusquely replied. "Come on!"
"Will I take the aul' bag for you?"

He got no reply. Cahal had headed off down the hill at speed, the thistles and nettles making little or no impression on his toughened bare feet. Séamus set off after him with angry shouts but there was no stopping now and he didn't catch up to his brother until they reached Butler's house where Old James sat outside the door soaking in the rays of the warm setting sun. The small house was neat enough but the signs were beginning to be seen of the curtailed ability of an old man living alone. He was nodding if not sleeping so the boys slowed and approached quietly, but he had seen them.

“Bhuochalee,” he greeted, “Dé bhur mbeatha,” and then realised that his was not their language and was about to change to the language of the Sassenach but Cahal answered,
“Go mairir i bhfad.”
This pleased the old man but he recognised the hesitancy.
“Éist to your grandmother, bhuochalee. The old things, sean rudaí…” and his voice trailed off and off and he was away in another time in another place and his stare damp-glazed his old eyes. Cahal and Séamus weren’t sure what to do but Old James shook his head and came back, back to them, back from long ago.
“Sa mhála, something old?”
“Sea! Yes! Yes!,” was all Cahal could say as he dug deep into the sack and pulled out the shield.

As he saw it emerge it repelled him slightly and he was momentarily annoyed that he hadn’t spent more time cleaning it up, but even as that thought ran through his head it was replaced by another, which saw all its apparent and hidden beauty and he didn’t speak the apology which came to his lips. Indeed had he considered speaking it he could not on seeing the change in the old man’s eyes when the rim appeared and the sack fell away and the shield presented itself.

“He put the holes in it,” Séamus blurted out and then moved to shelter behind Cahal afraid lest he had let him down. It didn’t matter. Old James hadn’t heard. He was holding the shield, a sacred and holy thing in his hands. He saw it, as it was now, as it had been, and both images fought for space in his mind and the original dominated and it was new and he was young and old age fell away and he was the warrior of the shining shield. The old head had to shake many times before the dominant image was replaced by the reality of now.

“Iontach! Breá! Ca bhfuair…Where did you find it?”

He listened intently as Cahal told the story with occasional unenthusiastic inputs from Séamus. The old man said nothing until he had finished.
“You have found the Sun Shield,” he began and he still held it and his eyes were fixed on it.
“The old people knew of three great treasures - Poll an Airgid, that is The Money Hole guarded by the supernatural bull. The second is the Claíomh Órga, Golden Sword buried beside the giant warrior on the hill yonder. The third and greatest is the Sun Shield and that is what you have found.”
“But who owned it?” Séamus interrupted.
“Éist, a mhic!” He pointed and continued. “The old fort has lost much of its glory. Once the walls were much higher. You can still see the lower steps. In it lived warrior kings who ruled over all these and surrounding lands. They were good to their people and served God well also. The great King, Brian Boru, visited and remarked on how fine a fortress it was. This made everybody proud. Níl a fhios if the shield was there then but it was always said that it was there it was kept. Many of the warriors followed King Brian to battle and many were killed. A bad time followed the king’s death and there was war and destruction in the land and the fort and its people suffered and the defence failed. The people were killed and the fort destroyed. I think that the shield was put in the water at that time. It could never fall into the hands of the enemy.”
“Then the shield is very old?” Cahal questioned.
“Older than old, maybe thousands of years, and now it is yours.”

“Father said that you would tell us what to do Mr. Butler, that you knew people…” Cahal left the remark unfinished. Old James handed back the shield. Cahal thought that it was more suited to the old hands than to his own. The old man and the old shield seemed to compliment each other. Séamus held the sack open and the shield slipped from sight.

“Sa chathair…. There’s a famous man who wrote a history book and has a big newspaper. His name is Mr. Morrison. Go to the city tomorrow and show him your shield. Tell him I sent you.”

CHAPTER SEVEN.

"Make sure to be back here by 4:00 o'clock," was Johnny Daly's admonition to the two boys as they left the Post Inn and moved uncertainly towards the city. For Séamus this was his first ever visit to the city and his excitement and expectation was huge, but there was also an element of fear and uncertainty and he moved in tandem with Cahal never more than a step behind. Not indeed that Cahal knew much about the city, but he had been there twice previously with his parents; something to do with a dowry for his aunt which needed a solicitor to draw up. He knew how to get to George's Street* and he had a good idea where No. 104 was; there he would find Mr. Morrison.

Church bells rang out across the city and the great spire of St. John's Cathedral pierced the sky and Séamus' mind. It was ten o'clock and the hustle and bustle of the day was well under way. A steady stream of horses and carts were moving in and out of the city. These were generally slow-moving and stayed close to the footpaths allowing clear passage to the carriages and coaches and cabbies and horsemen who moved at a much faster pace. The people they were meeting were all well dressed and hatted and in the beginning Séamus saluted shyly but got stares instead of benedictions.

"Why won't they salute us?" he wanted to know and Cahal explained that it was because they didn't know them.
"If they knew what we have here in the aul' bag, they'd salute us," and his voice rose in defiance and he saluted the next person, a portly, elderly man and this time he got a response which shocked him more than the lack of.

---

* now O'Connell Street.

"Two young men from the country, I see. Where are you from?" and his tone was friendly.
Séamus gulped and blurted out, "We're from Lough Gur, sir."
The gentleman rested his weight by leaning with both hands on his walking-cane.
"Then you are lucky," he said. "I only wish I could see it again. I was there many times when I was a young man and saw many objects recovered from the lowered waters. Often then I walked the hills and saw the beauty, a strange and wondrous beauty, which, I imagine is nowhere else on earth. You are lucky indeed. Are ancient objects still being found?"

Séamus stretched towards the sack but Cahal intercepted and answered.
"The odd bit, sir, but not at many as before. We had better be going. God bless you, sir."

He released Séamus' shoulder and raised his hand to forehead to salute. Séamus did likewise and they set off. Looking back they saw the old man still standing and watching them.
"Don't tell anybody what we have," and Séamus understood the tone but further distraction was not far away.

"Look! Look!" he shouted. Along the street came a funeral. It was the plumes, the black plumes on the horses' heads, swaying gently in time with each step that had caught his attention. The hearse was elaborate beyond belief and the black-clad, black tall-hatted driver and his companion were of the gravest visage. This time both were dumbfounded. At home the simple coffin was nearly always carried on a cart and even more often on neighbour's shoulders.

"Bless yourself and come on!" Cahal whispered urgently. Things were really getting out of hand. Three great buildings stood apart and each had sinister connotations.
"That's the lunatic asylum," Cahal pointed out. "And that one is the jail."
They were on their left-hand side and filled the mind with frightening images but the third, which was a hospital, became more real and frightening when the door opened and out came a blood-spattered porter pushing a trolley. A ruddy-faced, bulky man with a twinkle in his eye, he had the most remarkable handlebar moustache and his thinning hair was parted straight down the middle and plastered on his head. He came towards the boys at high speed and they stopped involuntarily and stood transfixed. Now he was beside them and the bright sun heightened the effect of the blood on his very white coat and his face and hands and the trolley were all spattered also. He stopped and went to the side of the trolley and leaned his elbows on it and now his eyes opened wide and he puckered up his mouth.
"A-a-a-r-h but he was a hardy one!" his voice boomed and he added cutting actions as he continued. "We had to cut his two legs off and his bones were so tough we broke two saws. There was blood flying in all directions and he was roaring and screaming and screeching," and he added like sounds. "Somebody had told him that his legs would be used for making soup for the dinner that day and it had upset him and he kept on shouting, "No soup! No soup!" We'd never have finished the job if I hadn't used my hammer when the surgeon's back was turned, and his voice lowered to a whisper and he laughed a blood-curling laugh that added to the shivers on the spines of the boys. "A tap on the side of the head and he was sound asleep," and he laughed some more.

All the while Cahal and Séamus remained frozen on the spot with a mixture of fear and disbelief. Legs failed to function even though they knew they should get away but this was an encounter rare and fascinating and demanding of a conclusion and it came. This seemingly wild bloody man smiled his puckered smile and slowly opened his hands like a conjuror or high priest and presented two bloodied palms, which he then moved to a gripping position on the covering on the trolley. Now his voice was taken to a higher pitch.
"I'm on my way to the butcher but you can have them for whatever you have in that old bag," and he swept the covering away and there lay two amputated legs.

That was it! They screamed in unison and ran and ran accompanied by the howling laughter. The screeching of pigs as they passed the pig-factory made them increase their speed. They finally stopped exhausted and breathless. Both were still somewhat shocked but Cahal was beginning to see some humour in the happening. This would be some story to tell the boys at home, but who would believe it? He was somewhat concerned for Séamus so he put his arm around his shoulder and gasped out.
"A Dhia, but wasn't he funny!"
"I'll never ate meat again," but he giggled as he spoke and Cahal knew that all was well. He tousled his hair, which he knew always annoyed him and saw the rising anger.

"Ar aghaidh linn," and it was indeed time to go. From across the street they were being watched by a group of ragged city children and even though none were as tall as Cahal there was about ten of them there and the bag had attracted their attention. Country people could sometimes be easy pickings. Cahal glared and it seemed to deter them but more likely 'twas the approach of a tall R.I.C. (Royal Irish Constabulary) man. Now Cahal was afraid that he might be asked to disclose the contents of the bag and this might take some explaining, so he tugged Séamus and ran on the opposite side of the street.

Now they were in Nelson Street.* Here the city was fully alive. The shops were of all kinds and the boys could have spent forever gazing at all the wonderful things on display in the windows. The street-sides were even more alive, where stalls competed and the vendors, mostly women of raucous voice, extolled their wares as the best available. Farmers had luscious vegetables for sale from carts and hens and ducks, eggs and butter, and bonhams in much demand in a city with a big pig production, members of which still enjoyed a street freedom.

"Toffee apples! I'm getting one," Séamus stopped short beside the station, "and I want to see the trains. You promised, Cahal."
"Two for a penny," the seller shouted as Séamus shyly put his penny in his hand. "They'll put hair on your chest. Straighten yourself up, young fella."

Séamus had recoiled on seeing that the fingers were missing and when he looked at the man's face he saw the eye-patch and the long ugly scar from forehead to chin. Recognising an audience he lifted the brim of the hat for a better display.
"Ye've heard of the Crimea, young fellas? We went out and fought the Russian. I was cut off from my company and there I was alone when who should come along only ten, maybe twenty Russian cavalry. Being a Limerick man I stood my ground. "Remember Limerick" I shouted like the Wild Geese of old, but they didn't understand and they attacked me. That was a mistake for them. Killed them all I did, and as they lay stretched on the ground, horses and all,

* now Parnell Street

and I taking a well-deserved drop of grog, didn't one of them who needed more killing take a swipe at me with his sword when I wasn't looking, and look what he did to me. Oh, you couldn't trust them, to do that to a man and he not looking. He'll not forget for a long time the second killing he got. Boys, I stood where thousands fell," and his proud military bearing which accompanied the telling quickly deflated when the porter at the gate of the station scoffed, "You did when you shook your shirt," and the laughter and anger mixed.

The toffee apples were delicious. The station was awesome. A train had just arrived from Dublin and it stood against the buffers at journey's end releasing steam and making sounds as if to attract attention and praise. It was getting attention anyway and it deserved it. It was a noble structure, an engineered giant which dominated everything even the newly-built station and the severely-proud-looking men who worked there. Proudest of all was the driver who was just now polishing the name-plate, BANSHEE, and above it, G.S.& W.R.*, while the oilman lovingly applied oil from a long-spouted can and the fireman, more black-faced than the other two stood admiring and drawing deeply on his pipe. Those who controlled these great engines deserved admiration and they made sure to wait about and bask in it.

"All the way from Dublin!" Séamus was so over-awed that he spoke in a whisper. This place was as sacred as a church. The only difference was the intense hustle and bustle of disembarking and movement of luggage on the platform. The passengers were all well dressed and prosperous-looking. Through the archway one looked out into the yard which was now cluttered with cabs and carriages and there was plenty of demand.

---

* Great Southern & Western Railway

"Come on! We'll never get there," Cahal tugged Séamus' jersey for the umpteenth time but he himself was so mesmerised that he almost needed someone to jerk him back into reality. "Soon I'll travel on one of them," but he didn't say it to Séamus.

Back on the street they were bombarded once more as a marching military band went past leading a column of marching soldiers. The display was spectacular but the 'red coats', for all their splendid appearance, were symbols of fear and oppression. They had been much in evidence in '67, just five years ago, and their treatment of some of the local men at Lough Gur and Grange after the attack on Kilmallock Barracks had been brutal and cruel and would be long remembered. Cahal had difficulty understanding why people applauded the passing band and soldiers but then a woman shouted,

"Johnny, Johnny! There's my Johnny. Wave to your mother, you brat!" which brought howls of laughter but no salute from Johnny only a broad wink.
"Fine young Limerick boys. God knows where they will be sent to now that they are ready for war. Wherever, they will be a credit to themselves and the Empire."
The man who spoke those words knew prosperity.

The Angelus bell jarred them back to reality. Where had the two hours gone to? Cahal and Séamus had long ago run out of words in this world of wonder but they would have much to talk about for a long time to come. They didn't stop as they walked by the railings of the very beautiful part where couples strolled and nannies pushed baby cars and took care of well-dressed youngsters from whom emanated shouts of joy and sometimes sorrow.

“This is the most important street in Limerick,” Cahal said as they entered George’s Street towards the top. The Crescent is a magnificent Georgian feature, which was not lost on the boys. The O’Connell Monument attracted but so did the rest of the buildings with their redbrick frontages, wrought-iron balconies, rails and basements and the most wonderful door furnishings. The church seemed oddly out of place.

There it was! No. 104! Bright gold lettering on the window declared that these were the offices of the LIMERICK REPORTER & TIPPERARY VINDICATOR.

“This is it!” Cahal whispered and they removed their caps as they climbed the steps.

CHAPTER EIGHT

Death-fires were common and the acrid smoke of burning flesh came in the wind. From his strong fort three miles south of the lake, Garaun could observe the death-happenings of the countryside and mostly took little notice except when looking north and knowing where and wondering who it might be. On this day he didn't know that the black smoke was his brother's burning flesh but he would before long when his messenger returned and he would be very saddened and angry. The breakdown of his relationship with his sister had deprived him of direct contact with his homeplace and this hurt and annoyed him.

When he had heard the full story his anger became more intense because Smet's killer was dead and revenge made impersonal. He knew of Esk's new role of companion and protector of Tana and the children. Being of noble family Smet's honour-price was five female bondswomen, but since his killer was dead and the situation was a war one, it was not possible to apply the rules of peacetime.

Garaun walked alone on the hillside. He wanted to formulate his own plans before he consulted with his brehon and military advisers. His people were prospering. Apart from minor skirmishes with travelling marauders peaceful relations had existed with neighbouring tribes for a long time. Not so with Nanda's people. For long her property had been under attack. He had not been able to help her because she had always refused his offers. This stubborn woman would bring about her own undoing and lead to the destruction of the most influential tribe in the area.

He noticed the first tinges of autumn colour touching the trees on the hillside under which some fat cattle sheltered from the strong midday sun. Beyond the corn was rich ripe and ready for harvesting. The tribe would be well provisioned for the winter, but these things were now only secondary. Smet seemed to call to him, to be calling all the time and he felt powerless and inadequate for all his power and position. He whispered to the spirits of the dead, to the good people within the hills and to the Christian God. Was his prayer being answered? Coming around the shoulder of the two-peaked hill (Cnoc da Adharc) he recognised the garb of the cowled and staffed figures. He felt and hoped that they were emissaries from the lake. Had Smet's death finally brought Nanda to her senses? Had Becan at last imposed his will on her? Would he himself get a chance at last to help his sister, to heal the rifts of many years? The monks were clearly moving with purpose. They would soon be here. He sat on a large stone and kept watch and the movement of the men and imagining their purpose lulled him into retrospect and the years tumbled back and images came flashing through his mind, of good times and bad, of war and peace, of life, of love, of death.

Garaun's thirty years had been spent on the hill of Aney. He had been fostered to the Ciarba clan. This was the fastening of the tribal link as Ciarba's son, Ciarb, had been fostered to the Gar clan of Carraig Aille. The consequences were predictable enough, but strange none the less. It didn't normally happen like this. The older people made the arrangements. In their wisdom they saw the binding of these two strong tribes would make a good union, a strong and safe entity. They had decided, and put it into effect, that the fostered sons would remain in their places of fosterage, marry a foster-sister and succeed to the rule of the tribe. At the time this would be seen as an unusual arrangement, infringing on many of the broad tribal rules, and requiring much discussion among the brehons of both clans, but it was seen as being wise and opportune because there had been a long period of aggravation between them and this was a way to resolve. It had worked very well.

Ciarb had been fostered at the lake and when his fosterage fee had expired, instead of returning to his own people, he and Nanda wedded and built a home within the great fort. Their marriage portions were generous and equal but in time it would be Ciarb who would be leader on the death of old Garbe or when he chose to relinquish the position. He had taken Ciarb under his wing from the beginning and set about making a leader of him. He had succeeded but many saw the real strength coming from Nanda. Meanwhile on Ainey, Garaun settled into a similar situation with the lovely Riac and all was well.

He heard the child come towards him and presumed the message she bore but did not speak or acknowledge. An intrusion, and he felt like turning and ordering her away but the timidity of her approach saved her from the harsh anger that welled up inside him. Anyway he might need it when he dealt with the monks.

"Speak, little one," he said without looking at her.
"Riac told me to find you and tell you that two monks are coming from the direction of the lake and she feels that they are coming to you," and her voice seemed to trail away as if fearing her message would aggravate, but his reply was gentle.
"Tell Riac to treat them hospitably until I come to them."
The child waited for some minutes and since no more was said she quietly left.

Death! Severer of relationships, ender of friendships, clothed in acceptability with the promise of after-life and re-birth, twin premises that help to salve part of the anguish of departure from life. Garaun allowed the faces of his dead to flow in a list through his mind and the list was long and distressing and when Smet became his focus, anger and frustration mixed and a blood-fury came on him and knowing that this could not be realised he fell on his knees and pounded the ground with his fists and tears flowed.

Time passed. This time Riac came herself. She didn't speak. She just touched his sleeve and he rose up and walked with her into the fort.

Both monks rose when Garaun entered. The greeting was formal and amounted to little more than a slight bowing of heads. Years of non-contact, years of strain and strained relationships, years of effort to resolve and fluctuating willingness and unwillingness, near solution and then a minute claim or difference to utter disruption and years of picking up pieces and rebuilding and as had happened so many times, failure yet again. The word minute did not apply to the longest-standing cause for difference - the ancient shield. Through it all however, Garaun and Becan's friendship never faltered.

"You know of your brother's death. We have sought his honour-price but the request has been ignored. The body of Smet's killer was collected by members of Vullen's tribe without interference, as respect for the dead demands. To them the request was made. Even though they did not have the authority to speak for Vullen and his tribe, they did mention that the honour-prices were equal and that the matter should end at that. Nanda will not agree to this. Vullen is the one who has harassed the lake people over many years and has caused serious damage to life and property. This time something must be done."

Becan continued to speak but Garaun's thoughts were scanning the years and recalling the difficulties, which had separated him from his family. The shield was the core of dissent. Ciarb had taken over the leadership from old Garbe and all was well for a number of years. The tribe prospered, but too often at the expense of other tribes less strong than themselves. As time passed Ciarb became more and more aggressive and less respectful of others' rights. The taking of cattle and slaves was commonplace and the victims usually responded to recapture their losses and this was done as far as possible without loss of life. Eventually it was not so with Ciarb. Time came when killing became his main intent and fear spread through the land. He paid the price. Vullen's people had been devastated by Ciarb's attacks. Then a young warrior, Vullen planned the removal of Ciarb and in a direct confrontation had killed him. No honour-price was paid. Nanda took over control of the lake-people.

Garaun mixed wisdom with ambition. Although he never doubted Nanda's ability to lead, he had hoped that she might consider herself vulnerable since Ciarb's excursions had considerably weakened her forces. She was young, still only in her twenties, and had responsibility for aged parents as well as children. Very likely she would marry again but the leadership would remain with Nanda if it didn't transfer to her new husband by agreement.

Silence brought him back.
"Is Nanda asking help from me? Does her pride allow?"
"As well as causing hurt, pride can also be hurt. Smet's death has been a terrible blow. Revenge alone will begin the

healing of that hurt and that is pride in different form, is it not?"

Away again! If only she had come after Ciaro's death. If this moment had been then. The tribes would have come together and dominated and he would have wielded power wisely. It hadn't happened and he knew that it was his pride was responsible then, and, of course, the shield. He had always wanted the shield, wanted to have it, to be its protector and guardian and holder. She hadn't come for help at that time, rather support in time of loss but he had made the demand the very moment the discussions were about to begin and his stubbornness met its match in Nanda's. Thus it had ended and what should have been an agreement of mutual benefit had finished in a storm of bitterness that had weakened both tribes and kept friends apart for years.

"Vullen is convinced that he had nothing to fear from you on Nanda's behalf. If he was to see that you were coming to her aid, he would see the wisdom in paying the honour-price and further bloodshed might be avoided."
"Is honour-price revenge?" he asked in surprise.
"If it is paid after being refused because of fear of repercussions as would be the case now," was Becan's answer.
"For Smet's killing I also need revenge and my revenge will be blood but one can be patient for that knowing that wheels turn and opportunities arise."
Garaun was tempted to ask,
"What of the shield?" but decided not to. Not yet! Maybe not at all! It shocked him that Becan could actually read his mind.

“The Sun Shield should be and must be a bond and it has to remain at the lake-fort,” and the words were weighted to disallow discussion.

Not for the first time Garaun regretted the impulsiveness of his past rejection and was not going to repeat it and he answered,
“Good Becan, carry happy tidings to my sister. I will visit tomorrow when the sun is high. Let us meet in the chapel of your monastery. Let the shield be there so that I may see it again and see if I can control my desire for it and my genetic right to it.”

Nanda hadn’t remarried but she did birth another child. That was Garvok, now a sturdy ten-year-old. There were no questions asked about paternity. Even as a woman, let alone chieftain, hers was the right to bear children. There were rumours as to who the father was. Becan was mentioned. If so then the secret was theirs. Independent as ever she refused to send Garvok for fosterage. He was to be educated by Becan and the monks. Her own warriors under her supervision would develop his fighting and hunting skills. She argued that this was the best way to prepare for the leadership which she asserted firmly would one day be his which would also be contrary to tribal code but that was for another day.

Becan had frowned at the reference to the shield but he said,
“May God bless you, Garaun. You have grown wise and wisdom will be rewarded.”

He then raised his hand in blessing, bowed in farewell and the two monks set out for the lakefort happily bearing good news.

CHAPTER NINE

"G'out a dat," was the response from the heavy-set clerk who sat at a high desk just inside the door. Cahal had knocked without reply and then finding the door unlocked had pushed it open and looked in.

"I want to see Mr. Morrison, if you please. I have something important to show him," Cahal said timidly. By now Séamus' head was in also.

"G'out you young rascals," the clerk shouted above the noise of the printing presses coming through from within and he lifted a heavy paper-weight as if to throw it at them.

Just then the door opened and in came a tall, grey-haired, long-bearded man. He had shed his coat but was impeccably dressed in silken waistcoat adorned with a gold watch-chain over starched high collar and bow tie. His trousers was grey pinstripe, his shoes shining black. Cuff links of gold and his shirtsleeves bore some ink spatters. He carried papers in one hand and a pencil in the other. His eyebrows immediately fascinated Cahal because they were jet black and incongruous between hair and beard. Forehead high and craggy, nose aquiline and eyes a piercing blue but face and hands held the delicate pallor of the indoors. There was an order and a sternness about this man. Could this be Mr. Morrison?

It was and he was walking past without even noticing the boys when Séamus called out.
"We want to see Mr. Morrison,"
The tall man stopped, turned his head slowly and looked down at Séamus.

"You are seeing him, young lad. Now you have seen him," and he began to walk away towards another door.

"Sir! Sir!" Cahal called, "Mr Butler told us to show you this and we have brought it in from Lough Gur."
"We found it in the bog," Séamus added.
Things changed immediately.

"My friend Old James. That wise man wouldn't send you in here to waste my time. Come with me."

Séamus turned and made a face at the clerk but regretted it at once when he realised that they would have to come out this way again.

With great care Cahal removed the shield from the sacking and laid it on the table. An audible intake of breath was Morrison's reaction. He stood and just gazed at it for what seemed an interminable time. Then he walked around the table looking carefully at it from all sides and angles, now kneeling as if to check the uniformity of the rings and bosses, at once admiring and seeking fault. He found none other than the two sickle holes. He had put on his spectacles and adjusted them regularly on his nose, sometimes taking them off as if closer inspection was better without them, othertimes using a lens as one would use a magnifying glass and then putting them back on again.

Finally he took it in his hands and scrutinised further and felt the weight and balance but Cahal didn't see the great love in his eyes that had been in Old James's but there was something else there which he didn't really understand. Morrison knew the significance of the shield. He had never seen such an example and was sure that it did not have an equal. It was perfect, the work of a master and very likely the most important artefact uncovered since the Ardagh Chalice, could rank with it and the Cross of Cong and other treasures in the Royal Irish Academy. But most of all he saw in it the prestige he would gain when he assembled his learned colleagues, showed them the shield and read his paper on it. That would be a moment to cherish. Could anyone then question his scholarship as some of the academics did?

"Were these holes in it when you found it?" he asked, trying to hide the excitement in his voice.
"Yes sir," Cahal replied, "but I made them when I struck it with the sickle."
"He was marking my jump," Séamus interjected but Morrison ignored him completely.

"As you can see it is in very poor condition and I'm afraid that the damage done by your careless use of the sickle has destroyed whatever value it might otherwise have had."
"But I didn't mean to damage it and had I not struck it, we would not have found it." Cahal's disappointment was turning into a plea as dreams of America began to fade away. Séamus didn't have the same regret.
"Mr. Butler said you would treat us fairly," Cahal tried again.

"Of course I will! Mr Butler's old eyes only saw its one-time glory but we have to be realistic and it is a badly damaged object and will never again regain its glory. It is very likely worthless but I will take it from you and give you a guinea for it."

"A guinea!" The boys exploded in disbelief.

“Bring it home, Cahal, bring it home!” Séamus called and inwardly he was pleased that he was not going to lose his brother to that far-off country.

Cahal stepped forward to take the shield from Morrison, but he held it firmly, clearly not wanting to part with it.

“I am a generous man,” he said, “ I will give you one pound, ten shillings for it and that is a very good price. Think how pleased your parents will be and how useful that money will be to them.”

In the silence that followed Cahal thought, “It’s my own fault. It’s too damaged. Nobody else will give me anything for it,” and he pushed Séamus, who was tugging at this coat, away from him. The hand that was still stretched towards the shield dropped to his side and he took a step backwards and Morrison knew that the shield was his.

How quickly dreams can shatter!
“Thirty bob,” thought Cahal, “Thirty pieces of silver,” and he felt sold also.
The shield was now Mr. Morrison’s. Maybe the price was right. Maybe the sickle damage ruined its value, just maybe. But all the while something was telling Cahal that he was being badly treated and it wasn’t just Séamus who had kept on saying “No! No! Bring it home.”

They didn’t even notice the clerk in the outside office as they passed through again followed by Mr. Morrison. At the door he said,
“Should you find other objects by your lake, bring them to me and I will pay you well for them,” which earned him a sharp look of disbelief from Séamus. If he noticed he chose to ignore it.

“Take my best wishes to Old James, Mr. Butler to you, and tell him to expect a visit from me within the month. Good day to ye, young fellows.”

That was that! The sights and sounds of George’s Street and the other streets passed over Cahal as they retraced their steps. His thoughts were on what now would not be. The fortune in the land of opportunity had slipped away, as had the plans and promises made.
“You shouldn’t have given it to him,” persistently from Séamus didn’t even gain a response.

Cups of tea and good thick beef sandwiches and cream buns in Flynn’s Tea Rooms. One of the waitresses was from home and she had many questions to ask. It was clear that she was lonely. They left her promising to tell many people that she was asking about them and one person in particular to which she shyly admitted.

They were in plenty of time for the longcar home. Outside the Post Inn the two horses had their nosebags on, tails and ears twitching against the flies. Somebody joked that Johnny Daly had his nosebag on also. He was inside having his pints, bantering with the city lads about the advantages of country life. Other passengers arrived and it was time to go. Johnny was a little unsteady and a good bit boisterous.
“What had ye in the aul’ sack this morning,” he called to Cahal and Séamus as the longcar headed out the Old Cork Road on its way to Bruff.
“That was my big black tomcat,” Séamus replied smiling broadly.
“We sold him for thirty shillings,” Cahal added.

The boys looked at each other and burst out laughing.

CHAPTER TEN.

There wasn't any preparation needed because the church was always ready to receive. Even so the monks made extra effort as if to acknowledge the importance of what was to take place. The church was the only stone structure other than the strong walls of the fort. Its best feature and source of great pride, visitation and admiration was the elaborately decorated entrance door. The work of a travelling craftsman monk, Omanes, he left fine examples of his skills, but most agreed that this was his masterpiece. Sometime later, having departed a monastery on the great lake of Derg to the north, carrying rich rewards for his labours, he was waylaid by robbers and his resistance cost him his life.

Good light shone in through the large window on the south wall and illumined the brightly coloured frescoes on the sanctuary wall of which a figure of Christ crucified was the centrepiece. The altar was of plain stone, was covered with a white cloth and candles burned in finely wrought silver candlesticks. The floor of the sanctuary was paved and seats for the monks backed each sidewall. Rails separated sanctuary from nave where the floor was of mud and the very few seats of rough timber, walls undecorated, yet beautiful in its simplicity. The bell-tower adjoined but was no more than twenty feet in height, a delightful and true replica of the full-sized monastic towers. From its top bells delivered notice of the passage of time, assemblies, danger and celebrations. It rang for life, it rang for death.

On this morning it rang to celebrate the return of one long absent, to announce his arrival and it pleased Garaun, hearing the bell as he passed Carraig Aille on his way to the monastery. He rode on a fine grey horse and his colourful cloak bespoke his position. His sword appeared from beneath. His company was of four mounted shield and spear-carrying warriors, grim of face, ever expectant of danger. The news was out that Garaun was returning and little groups had gathered by the wayside and the cheer rose and was acknowledged with salute and smile.

Once he stopped. The old man was wrinkled with age, bent double with aching bones. This man had been his father's servant, more friend than servant and Garaun recognised him and stopped in a flood of youthful memories

"God bless you, old Arra. To see you fills me with joy," he said gently and bending down held the old man's gnarled hand.

"It is time you came back to us, Garaun. Help is needed and it is from you it should come," and his voice croaked in antiquity and people looked in amazement because Arra hadn't spoken a word for well over a year. Garaun dismounted and embraced the old man.

"It is so good to see you, Arra. My father always valued your advice and help and so will I. Coming along I noticed the ravages and I know that the tribe is hard-pressed. Much will depend on Nanda."
"Be easy with her,' Arra croaked again. "She has had her trials and troubles and pride alone sustains her. You cannot take that from her. Don't try!"

He didn't say another word and as far as is known he never spoke again even though he lived for over two more years. 'The day that Arra spoke' was more commonly used than 'the day that Garaun came to the monastery.'

Monks went about their business as if unaware of the visitor as Garaun entered through the open gate. A furtive peep, perhaps from the shelter of their cowls, no more. He handed the reins to his servant. The doorway was a magnet drawing him towards it. As a child he had watched Omanes create it, awe-stricken by the skill which could produce such perfection. He stopped at the doorway and touched each order lovingly and reverently, spanning the years, gone forever. The shield sprang to his mind, claiming its place in thoughts of beauty, and a strange realisation struck Garaun, and he thought,
"The doorway belongs here and no place else. So does the Sun Shield! In my discussions with Nanda let me remember that."
He fought to control the rejection of the thought as it boiled up within him.

The third thing of beauty was Nanda. She knelt before the altar. A beam of sunlight entered through the small window above the doorway catching her red hair. He cherished the moment. He knew that she was aware of his presence.

"Let him wait," she thought to herself.

"Let her make the first move," was his thought.

"Come," said Becan, sensing the growing pride in both, and they came because both wanted to.

It was not to be the warm or even the tentative embrace of siblings long parted, rather a cold formal meeting of leaders with needs, and Nanda's needs were the greater. For her it was an urgent search for a strong ally and while she would have to pay a price, it needed to be as little as possible. She was well aware of her diminished state in both tribe and

property. The toll of the past years was high on cattle, slaves and warriors. Garaun was coming from a position of strength, having successfully defended and extended his territory, grown rich in stock and slaves, mostly through wise trade rather than warfare. When warfare was needed he was able for that also. And so the brother and sister were meeting on unequal, very unequal terms. His position was secure, but she, in her straitened situation, wanted help to restore the greatness of her tribe so that it would be a worthy tribe to hand over to her son when the time would come. The shield could be her trump card; Smet's killing a mutual binding matter.
"Sister and brother, come close together and may the good Lord bless and guide you both."
As he spoke the words, it seemed as if Becan was intoning one of the many prayer-calls of the day. Indeed he hoped that the dignity of collective prayer would be part of the discussion to follow, and that the dignities of the participants would remain intact, his own included.

Nanda knew that coming from the weaker position it would be wise for her to begin proceedings.

"Becan says, and rightly, that I need help, and he has made the contact with you. I am pleased that you have come. I am, and have always been unhappy that you allowed us to be distanced from one another. We will blame each other. You will see your rights usurped by me, and your anger will mostly centre on the shield. It is ours in our sharing of blood, but it is mine as leader of the people of Car. Yours are the people of Aney."

The very mention of the shield raised Garaun's hackles but he had promised Becan that it would not be an issue. Still he did not close his mind to the possibility of acquiring it or of even having occasional access to it. He would delay any mention of it.

"Smet's killing is more of a blood matter. In your church, Becan, I know I should not speak of revenge, but I speak of it, because outside of this place I think of little else. It is a duty to my murdered brother which I will honour."

Becan raised his hand but Garaun continued, speaking now to Nanda.

"I take no pleasure in your weakened position. In the glory of this tribe I always take pride, in its decline I am saddened. The one good thing is that the decline has undermined your independence and your pride and has given me a chance to return and renew our friendship."

"The fault was yours, Garaun," Nanda interrupted, "you who would not accept that the guardianship of the shield, the Sun Shield, was my God-given right as leader of this tribe."

"The shield has more to do with family than tribe. Our family has been its guardians, its keepers, for as long as memory can span. It belongs to family rather than tribe and our father once commanded me to care it after his death. But let that be for the present"

Becan stood beside them and watched the changing emotions, the rising anger, the twinges of regret for lost years and lost friendship, the realisation of the folly of stubbornness, the need now for mature friendship and dependence on each other. Garaun was giving and Nanda's mood was changing to preparing her to accept. If he demanded the shield, she would revert to her original position, but she didn't want to do that. She hoped she

would not have to. She had no cattle to offer, not enough slaves to give any away and anyway she knew that Garaun was rich in all of these. Yet if he were to give, she would also have to give. It was an impasse for her. What would he offer? What would he ask, demand? She looked to Becan for help and he responded.
"Garaun, you have come to help, so offer your help, and if there is a price to be paid waive it in generosity or let it be of a kind that will no further hardship your sister. I see a great bond being re-established between you and Nanda, a bond that was always there but was clouded in the responsibilities which life imposed on you both. May God give you guidance."

In the ensuing silence a cloud crossed the sun and the inside of the church darkened. Was this an omen? Nanda felt her heart flutter slightly but then the cloud passed over and she saw that her brother's face was unclouded and there was a gentle smile on his lips. At that moment she fully realised how helpless she was. Her will to fight on alone weakened. Suddenly she felt the burden of all the responsibilities and decision-making that she had carried for so long Before she knew it, her strong stubborn pride had dissipated and she heard herself saying,
"I need your help, Garaun. I need your help."

These simple words from his beautiful much-admired sister fell on willing ears. Garaun had long hoped for reconciliation, but he would have preferred had she come to him from a position of strength. In a way it didn't matter because he had made up his mind that he was not going to take advantage. At that same moment what seemed a solution to the Sun Shield problem flashed into his mind.
"I will help you, Nanda," he said. "I will put you under my protection, will be your ally and let all the surrounding tribes

know this. An attack on you will be an attack on me. An injury to you will be an injury to me. You will share my revenge on Vullen and that will come when he least expects it or sooner if he should attempt plunder again and I will supply the bait."

She could scarcely believe her ears. There had to be a catch, a price.
Garaun continued.
"I will re-people your fort by sending you thirty warriors. They will come with their families and possessions, they will build their houses on the valley slope north of the fort. With them will come tradesmen, who, with the assistance of your remaining tradesmen, will rebuild and strengthen and occupy the second fort on the hilltop, which will be eventually the last line of defence. To this I need access and the right to live there for a period in each year. Will you allow this?'
She nodded and said "Yes!" even though a voice within was saying,
" He is trying to take over my position. He is establishing a foothold for that purpose. And yet he is sorting out my difficulties. I must agree."
"To see to the needs of the increased numbers you will need more slaves. They will also be needed to care for the thirty cows, which they will bring."
"This is too good," thought Nanda. "Should he ask for the shield I would almost be tempted."
But she knew that she would not, could not ever hand over her guardianship. Becan was pleased also and listened intently.
"A price? There is a price. There has to be a price. The warriors will remain with you. They have other skills also which will prove useful. Each year for the next four years you will return ten calves to me, strong calves at weaning

time at year's end. For the five years following you will return ten child slaves each year. Do you, Nanda, agree?"
"You are most generous, Garaun, and I am pleased to comply with your terms." Somehow she knew there was more to come and she waited and hoped.
"I have always claimed that the guardianship of the shield should have been mine. I could insist but I know that you would not yield on that and I have promised Becan that I would not make that demand. However, when I visit the fort each year I want access to the Sun Shield and the right to keep it in the fort during that time, or for some of the time, at least. This is not an unreasonable request, you will agree?"
He looked at Becan and Nanda as they looked at each other and he knew that both would agree. But the strong hand had still one card to play and he resolved to play it from his now strong position.
"Your son, Garvok, will one day lead this tribe. That, I know, is your choice, as his birth was your choice.' Becan shuffled uneasily. 'You have also chosen to keep secret the name of his father and you do not have to answer to his father about his upbringing."

There was something in the posture and expression of both Becan and Nanda that confirmed what was suspected. He was indeed speaking to both parents of the child. Neither spoke so he continued.
"You have chosen to ignore the ancient rules of fosterage through which the young are prepared for manhood and leadership. You are depriving Garvok by your selfishness. If he doesn't learn independence and skills of leadership in war and peace he will not be fit to lead."
"No!" she spat out the word. "Never!"
Becan put his arm around her and held her tightly.

"All I have offered I withdraw unless Garvok comes to live with me in Aney. From me he will learn what he needs to know. With me he will be safe and well-cared for, and he will perfect the skills of life."

There was no way out. Her pride took a fall, a tear rose to her eye and she put her head on Becan's shoulder and sobbed her assent.

CHAPTER ELEVEN.

"No luck in those old things," was his mother's retort when she was finally told about the shield.

"That dacent man gave you a good price for it, bail ó Dhia air. 'Twill pay for a suit of clothes and a pair of boots for you for the winter."

His father didn't make any comment but Cahal saw the anger in his silence when he heard how they had got on with the rich newspaperman in Limerick. Séamus was the only one who was happy and for weeks he laughed at his story about selling the old tom-cat.

Old James Butler was furious.

"A bhuachaill," almost shouting, "Rinne an fear sin… That man treated you badly and in treating you badly he treated me badly also. Mo bhrón! But I will let him know of my displeasure."

He rose and went to the dresser and took down a sheet of writing paper, a bottle of ink and a pen. He came to the table and wiped a corner of it with the sleeve of his coat.

"'Nois, Cahal, sit down and write the words I speak."

Cahal did as asked, sat at the table, surveyed the sheet of paper, seeing the layout of the finished letter in his mind. Then he took up the pen and checked the nib, opened the inkbottle and dipped, scraping off the surplus on the rim of the bottleneck. He wanted to do this well, didn't want any blots and was pleased when the old man gave him a piece of blotting-paper, after which he returned to his chair by the fire. In the moment of silence that followed Cahal was conscious of the ticking of the wall-clock and the purr of the cat on Old James' lap.

"Scríobh an seoladh agus an dáta… the address and the date," and Cahal began…

Lough Gur,
Holycross,
Bruff,
Co. Limerick.
27th August 1872.

Mr. Morrison, Sir,
I hope this letter finds you well, as I am well myself, thank God. Yes! I am well but age has taken from me my ability to write and so I am dictating these words to a young man with whom you have recently become acquainted. He is Cahal Hayes of Lough Gur.

The passage of time, which caused my hand to tremble, was temporarily reversed on the evening that young Cahal brought his great find to me. I speak of the Sun Shield, the greatest treasure that Lough Gur has yet yielded up. The Sun Shield has been the subject of more lore and discussion than all the thousands of artefacts found after the lowering of the lake and since. The stories were passed from generation to generation; the story of the master-smith who made it, helped by the Fairy Queen, Áine; how the tribe of Gar became its guardian; the story of the warrior-princess Nanda, whose son, Garvok, made the supreme offering of the shield to the spirits of the water in a desperate and despairing effort to bring the spirits to his aid as his fort succumbed to the terrible onslaught of his enemies. Since then the Sun Shield, which holds the key to many mysteries of the circles and standing stones, has remained hidden in the Small Lake. This is the story that has been told over the years and it was always said that one day it would be found, and it was further said that the finder would prosper and travel far.

Mr. Morrison, the Sun Shield is a treasure and will stand beside the wondrous Ardagh Chalice and Tara Brooch. It is much more ancient than either of those, is crafted with comparable skill, is perfect in design and purpose, and the knowing eye does not see the marks of the sickle. Do you see them, Mr. Morrison?

These words are the anger of an old man who feels betrayed. It was I who chose you to be the one to have the honour of first seeing, and acquiring this famed artefact. You, sir, abused my trust, insulted the Sun Shield, your own distinguished position and my young friend, to whom I guaranteed your integrity.

I sincerely hope that the financial results of young Cahal's visit to you are but an error of judgement rather than an attempt to take advantage. If that is so, then I apologise to you as soon as this injustice is corrected. Until then I do not want you to visit me. If you feel that I am the wrong one, then see fit to immediately return the Sun Shield. Cahal will return to you your paltry purchase price and I will direct him elsewhere. If I were in a position to properly reward him for his find, then I would do so, look at the shield once more and return it to the lake, in the hope that it would remain there until more enlightened times.

I remain, Mr. Morrison,
Yours in disillusionment

The intensity of the contents left Cahal drained, but the words jumped back at him from the page and he knew that he was honoured to have this old man as a friend. He was pleased that the letter was neat and orderly and free of blots, even though he had written faster then he had ever done to keep pace with the anger of the old man. He didn't notice James rising from his chair; a touch on his shoulder and he rose and James sat at the table, took the pen and signed the letter with a flourish with a hand that did not tremble.

Cahal was particularly careful as he addressed the envelope, wishing that he could embellish the capitals in the same fashion as James did with the J and B in his signature. The final full stop, the careful application of blotting paper and the job was done. One last look at the letter, a look of admiration and wonder, the folding and the placing in the envelope. As he licked the flap, some gum stayed on his tongue and he grimaced and tried to remove it by scraping his tongue on his top teeth, the sound reaching his ears internally. Done! A moment of silence! Old James sat staring at the hearth where the turf fire was burning low. The white ash was waiting to be raked aside, turf to be added and the bellows turned. The kettle on the crane had gone off the boil, but would quickly spout steam again from its blackened body when the added fuel was blown to heat. The bastable, which had been used to bake the cake of bread on the window-sill, was at the far side. His dog lay with paws almost in the ashes. The cat came back in, slyly looked about and slithered onto the old man's lap, assured of a welcome.

He had already taken the money from the small cloth bag which was always hidden somewhere inside his shirt.

"Seo dhuit," and then, "Here, Cahal, take this and go to the post office and send the letter to Mr. Morrison."
He handed Cahal a shilling.

The lakefront was quiet. On the water the ducks looked scraggy in their moulting, now confined to the water, temporarily without flight until the onset of their new flight feathers, the reproduction of the year done. This part of the lake was the domain of one family of swans. They were all together beside the crannog (man-made island), the grey of the five cygnets in unfavourable contrast to the brilliance of the parents' plumage. However they were quickly developing in size and in dignity and grace of movement. Cahal knew that they would soon be driven from this part of the lake, to find their own mates and territory elsewhere, and the cob and pen would rule again, alone until next season. Now the water was calm but the shore was flecked with foam from yesterday's strong westerlies.

When the sound reached his ears it brought his brisk walk to an abrupt stop. He had just passed the limekiln and he could see her standing by the Spectacles. The song she was singing he knew to be 'The Coolin', the haunting love-song composed by a native of the parish, Fr. Ailbe O'Hanley, over a hundred years before. Mary Bresnan had the best voice in Lough Gur and for miles around. He felt a shiver on his spine as he listened, and the thought struck him that it was well that this wasn't happening in darkness because it would then have been a fairy voice, a voice from the enchanted land. There were other thoughts also, as he stood enthralled. The stirrings of love had begun in the young man and all that love was directed towards Mary. As she finished the song, she slowly turned about and seeing that she had an audience her hand went to her mouth as if to close off the sounds that were already gone. Just as quickly she raised her head, tossing her red hair defiantly.
"What are you looking at, Cahal Hayes?"she taunted.
Cahal chose not to reply but to allow this moment of beauty and wonder to implant deeply in his mind, to be recalled again and again.
"Well?" she shouted down.
"Come here," he called and she skipped down the Staighree, trying to slow down with small slapping steps of her bare

feet, speeding towards him, then turning her lithe body and avoiding him at the last moment; laughing as she went past, then pivoting to a stop.
"Where are you going?" she asked.
"I'm going to the post office to post this letter for Mr. Butler."
As he held up the letter she snapped it out of his hand and ran to the water's edge, and held it over the water.
"Cahal Hayes, if you don't promise to buy me a square of toffee, I will drop it in the lake."
"Ah, Mary!" was all he could say, and then pleaded, "Give it back to me. I promise."

Eyes sparkling with delight and roguery, dimples clearly defined in her smiling face, she stretched out the letter and as he took it she ran helter-skelter along the shore, laughing heartily.
"Don't forget," she shouted back. "I'll be waiting!"
He watched her for a while and then set off towards Knockfennel, but she stayed in his mind and became part of his America dreams.

CHAPTER TWELVE.

The children stopped their playing on the lakeshore. Esk sat in his boat by the Carraigeen with his spear frozen in the air. A stillness came upon the creatures of lake and land, their own sounds muted by the perfect human sound of Tana's voice. She hadn't sung since her lamentation for Smet. Was the heartache easing? The first notes were low, almost testing, and sad. Little by little she entered the full flush of song and her voice carried on the water and reached the distant shore, and moved left and right on to the hills and the hearers stopped from their work and the wonder rested on them and restored them. Some understood and 'nod-acknowledged.

"Tana is healed!" was the message and they were glad. The wicked old hag of the Rua Suidhe (Red Seat) heard her also. "It didn't take the eel-fisher long to fix her," she hissed.

She couldn't have known that Tana was pregnant but Tana did and that was the real reason for ending her mourning. "I must bear this child happily. I must carry him with strength and pride and Smet will live again in him."

Whenever he came to her mind she looked towards the top of the northern hill. That's where Smet's remains rested, his poor dead body now crouched to the foetal position by semi-cremation. From there he could watch over the lake and land until his re-birth, hopefully in the child in her womb. His spirit was elsewhere, now with the gods in their world, now free about the land.

The song ended, the world released its breath and things reverted. Esk lowered his arm, so moved by the moment that he wasn't able to return to the kill. He remained still and in reverie he scanned his and Smet's great friendship, of happy youth spent together and their wonderful experiences as they matched each other in skills of prowess in sport and hunting. Never to be forgotten was the debt he owed to Smet and with the thought came anger. He had failed to repay. He had not saved his friend's life and the debt would remain unpaid. A dark cloud of despair came over him as the details flashed through, exploding in his mind.

Whenever he walked in the forest after rain the scent of the crushed leaves underfoot brought back the memory of that day. The heavy rain had kept them impatiently indoors all morning and as it began to clear Smet called to Esk from the shore.

"Come on, Esk, we'll go hunting," as he shot a flat stone from his catapult and sent it skimming on the water, making five decreasing leaps before sinking. Without speaking Esk chose a stone from the shore of the crannog and did likewise but managed six leaps. Smiling wryly he moved to the little boat and as he touched land said,

"We'll cross to the other side. Jump in!"

Staunch fourteen year old friends seeking adventure, fearless and oftimes foolish. As they sped across the water Esk took the boat to the point of capsize. Somebody of lesser skill would have lost it but not Esk; nor did he frighten his friend, or if he did no complaint was made, but it would be remembered on land. On the steep face of Knockfennel, Smet's strength put him ahead of Esk and he had no hesitation in pushing Esk repeatedly, that was until the fish spear was pointed and the words of warning added.

Over the hill and into the forest that covered the high ground at the foot of the hill. They had decided to go to the river,

hunting as they went, and there Esk could use his fish-spear for salmon and trout with his excellent skill. It was as they ran through the forest that Esk smelt the crushed leaves underfoot and this fresh after-rain smell would always remain with him and remind him of Smet and the happenings of that day. A cock pheasant was disturbed from his feeding and ran across their path. They went in quick pursuit with catapults primed. The pheasant stayed on the ground and seemed safe among the trees. The brilliance of his plumage was heightened in the sunbeams. The boys were close behind when he rose with a defiant crowing. They stopped, aimed and both stones connected and the pheasant fell awkwardly to the ground. They cheered in their delight and slapped each other's backs. Smet ran and picked up the bird, tied the legs with a thong which he slung over his shoulder and attached to his belt. He felt the body heat through his thin clothing. His were the first spoils.
'You can carry the fish, but you'll have to catch them first.' Esk smiled in reply.

They reached the river in which there was a good run of water after the rain, but it had not as yet turned muddy. Stealthily they approached the ford that was west of the riverbank monastery. They didn't want to be seen if possible because they were entering the lands of Vull with whom the tribe was in a state of continuous aggression. The pull of the water was strong and they clutched for each other as they stumbled on the slippery stones. At the far side they ran along the bank and reached the shelter of a grove. They hid when a monk approached, visibly tired having trekked between the two monasteries on the river. He needed his staff to help him along.

"All clear!"

They moved into fishing positions. They lay face down on the riverbank motionless. Esk held his spear above the surface waiting for a salmon to come within range. Smet was less ambitious and was trying to practice the old art of tickling a trout. The sun sparkled on the water and the warmth of the day and the gurgling water sounds lulled Smet to impatience in a short time. Speech wasn't allowed so he rose quietly and strolled down the riverbank. Time passed. He was pissing against a tall tree when he heard firstly, the shout of exultation and he knew that Esk had impaled a salmon. This was followed by a shout of pain, from Esk also, and a shout of triumph from another. Smet raced in the direction but instinctively stayed in cover.

From the grove he saw Esk lying on the bank with blood streaming from his head, the salmon on the ground beside him and the strong youth going to them, catapult still in hand. Smet realised what had happened and knew that Esk was hurt and unconscious. The youth approached Esk and as Smet watched in stunned amazement, he put his foot under Esk and pushed him into the river, chuckling loudly as he did so. Catapult? At his feet Smet saw a stout oak limb almost like the staff the monk had been carrying. He picked it up and ran at the youth, who turned on time to avoid being struck on the head, but it landed on his shoulder breaking his collar-bone. With a loud cry Smet struck again and the blow landed on the youth's chest and with a scream of pain he fell back into the river. Smet cast the limb aside and ran along the bank, shouting for Esk. He saw the inert body being carried along by the current and knew that he must act quickly. Ahead was a cut on the bank to which the cattle came to drink. He raced there and wading in caught Esk and pulled him ashore. Spluttering and coughing Esk regained consciousness. The jagged cut on his forehead oozed blood and his eyes were glazed but the words came.

“Smet! Smet!”

Now he heard himself calling out the same word and tears were running down his cheeks. His boat had drifted out in the lake and his name was being called. It was Tana. The moment passed and he realised where he was.
“Esk! Esk!” she called. “Nanda has sent word that she wants to see you as soon as possible.”

CHAPTER THIRTEEN

Mary had been to the post office in Holycross.
"Who are you now?" Mrs Mack had asked.
"Mary Bresnan from Lough Gur."
"Your brother is handy with the pen?"
"He is!"
"The gift!"
"Some would say so."
"And you're the singer?"
"Some would say so."
"None of that cheek out of you, young one," and Mrs. Mack's thin lined face hardened in fleeting annoyance.

Mary was always amused by her appearance. The thin face, strealish white hair, spectacles perched low on her nose, inside the barred counter like a bird in a cage. Curiosity was the hallmark of her occupation and she gathered as much gossip as possible and spread it about properly embellished. The content of letters wasn't safe either and she had been known to inform a person what it contained before handing over a letter to them. But her clear blue piercing eye had a roguish sparkle to it and her quick tongue and readiness to share everybody's news, good and bad, and the strong smell of tobacco were redeeming features. The clay pipe was always with her, in her apron pocket or on the counter, when it wasn't in her mouth. Her few teeth were heavily tobacco stained and a cloud of smoke hung over her in the dimly lit office. She lit the pipe and dragged on it; it wheezed and quenched.
"Bhlast you for a useless yoke," she complained as she struck another match and tried again.
"Do you know Mr. Butler?"
"Of course I do."

"There's a letter here for him, a letter with money in it!"
"Do you want me to take it to him?"
"I do."
"I will, …..if you give me sixpence!"
"Oh, 'tis you're the cheeky one, Miss," and she glared through the bars but then decided that she had met her match and she grinned her scarce-toothed smile and beckoned Mary closer with a conspiratorial shake of the head.
"There's money in it, and it's from a newspaper man in Limerick and it could be good for young Cahal Hayes. Now will you take it?"

Thoughts came together for Mary. She remembered the day, now almost a month ago, when she had met Cahal by the lake. He had said that he was posting a letter for Mr., Butler. Could it have something to do with the Sun Shield? She had heard the story of the 'old cat' and how disappointed Cahal had been. He really wanted to go to America.
"I will, Mrs. Mack! I will take it to him."
Mrs. Mack looked at the back of the envelope for a moment to make sure that it had been properly resealed. Then she slipped it out to Mary, and as she took it two squares of toffee followed and the roguish grin.
"Bye, Mrs. Mack! Thanks, Mrs. Mack!" and she was out the door and away. Instead of crossing the fields she decided to go home by the road. It was longer but she would be passing the field near the Cross where the boys played hurling. She might meet Cahal. She would tell him about the letter but not a word about the contents.

Cahal! Cahal! Cahal! The name would not leave her mind and as she sucked on the toffee she thought again of the evening of the letter and he had brought her the toffee and she had made sure to be by the lakeshore on his return. She began to sing 'The Coolin' very softly and stopped abruptly when she realised that she was passing the graveyard. She knew the woman who was kneeling and weeping beside the fresh grave that held her husband. Mary prayed for him and for her own relations buried within. She didn't feel fear when passing the Giant's Grave but felt a chill when passing the Rock of the Lies because it was a favourite haunt of the little people and they had always to be treated with respect. And then a great feeling of loneliness came upon her, which she did not understand.

'He is going away and will never come back,' and the words raced through her mind again and again.

"Why am I thinking like this?"

She spoke the words aloud. But she did not have an answer, nor did she realise that the first stirrings of love had begun within her; her carefree childhood was in transition.

She didn't hear the horse and cart 'til it rattled around the bend, the horse trotting briskly. Cahal was driving and Séamus was with him.

'Stop!' Séamus shouted.

A shyness had come on Cahal when he saw Mary which prevented him from taking the normal action of stopping and offering a lift since they were going in the same direction. Without salutation Mary said,

"'Tis I have the letter this time," and she held it up and, strangely impelled by shyness, blurted out, "and it's from a rich man in Limerick and there's mon…."

Just on time she remembered Mrs. Mack, but she had said enough to stir the curiosity.

"Is it for Mr. Butler?"

"Yes, it is! Mrs. Mack asked me to bring it to him."

"We'll take you, won't we, Cahal." Séamus said and Cahal gladly agreed.

"Jump up!" he called.

The boys were sitting on either side in the front of the cart. Mary was now on the back, looking backwards, bare feet dangling. The iron-rimmed wheels and the shod hooves were muffled on the dust road as the cart lurched on the potholes and the loose stones on the hill caused the horse to slip, and as Cahal steadied him with a tight rein, Séamus pointed to the marsh and called back to Mary,
"'Twas down there we found the aul' shield."
Soon it would be sunset and the boys would miss out on the hurling. Their friends were in the field as they turned the Cross and the threesome were greeted with cat-calls and remarks to which Séamus had plentiful reply while Cahal again felt shy.

Mary knocked at Old James' door. The dog barked and the old man called,
"Tar isteach! Tá sé ar oscailt! Come in!"
Mary gave him the letter and was immediately rewarded with a sixpence. Then James came out to the fading light, greeted the boys, opened the letter and read with seeming difficulty. Cahal expected that he would be asked to read it for him but he wasn't asked and he watched the old man's face and saw emotions fleeting from anger to sadness, to annoyance and finally to a certain satisfaction.

"A anam don diabhail!" he snorted, "but we got him, the aul' miser," and holding a slip of paper aloft in triumph added, "and this is a draft for £8 -10 - 0 for you, Cahal. It still isn't a fair price but it is much nearer the value. Here, a bhuachaill!" and his tone became sad,
"I suppose it will take you away from us."

CHAPTER FOURTEEN

Before returning to Aney Garaun visited the fort where a feast of anticipated celebration had been prepared. He and Nanda walked slowly there from the monastery finding that the friendship of years ago had only dulled into a state that awaited recall. They spoke of parents and friends, of servants and playmates, of adventures and misadventures, and it was all good. His heart pounded with excitement as they approached the entrance. He had always intended to change the entrance to Aney to be exactly like Carraig Aille. Oman had prompted the design as he had worked on the doorway of the church, but he had not executed it.

The ground area was divided into two sections, one of which was cobbled and the preserve of the entering and exiting cattle; the other, paved and a little higher and intended for human use. And each species remained on its own side.
"Quite ingenious!" was Garaun's admiring thought.

The thick walls were recessed in the middle so that the stout doors were safely stowed when open during the day. The other feature of steps leading to the top of the surrounding wall had not been Oman's idea but they added greatly to the completeness of the fort and made it distinctive and speeded access in times of attack.

"This was the home of great leaders and is more than fit for great leaders and it will entertain them again. It deserves great leaders," but he did not speak the words.
What he said was,
"Considering your ill-fortune of past years your fort is in fine repair."

"Smet made sure that it would be so. His skills and constant cajoling of people to keep clean and his dedication to seeing that everything was properly maintained is the reason why. But he is no longer with us," and her voice checked, caught in the emotion of deep loss.

The welcome given him was cautious enough. This was the brother who refused to help his sister, their leader, in her difficulties. He was the one who wanted the Sun Shield! What right had he? The right of the powerful! And he could have attacked and taken, which wouldn't have been unusual among siblings in this war-torn land.

"I met old Arra as I approached. He asked me to help you."
"He hasn't spoken for years. The loss of our tribal prestige must mean much to him."
"Well he might ask, more friend than servant to father for so many years, but wasn't he the cranky one?"
"He treated me well but I know he often left the mark of his hand on you, but you did deserve it."
Garaun laughed easily in remembering.

Smiling, Nanda led him through the entrance and the occupants bowed in welcome. His troop had entered the higher fort from which loud laughter was floating down. No reticence there! Those fighting men knew each other. As yet they would not know that bonds were being forged between the tribes, and that some of them would be coming here to remain permanently and help defend Nanda and her territory.

Nanda knew how to divert attention from the strain of Garaun's presence. She nodded to her maidservant who immediately entered the house, returned and handed Nanda her ceremonial mace. When she held it above her head all knew that the Sun Shield was to be displayed and great anticipation lit the eyes of all and Garaun was momentarily forgotten. He also, had forgotten everything except the Sun Shield. It had been years, years of waiting. He could hear his heart beating in his ears; he felt his breath increasing to fast short intakes; perspiration made his hands cold and clammy. The years rolled back. Was he young? Was he old? Would he see his parents? His old servants? His young friends now grown old? Two youths stepped forward, ready. This was their turn. They had stripped to the waist and their bodies were oiled to shine in the sun when they held the Shield. He had done this also. When? With whom? He was back in his time of youth, a small boy and the expectation now was as the expectation then. The smells of cattle, of food cooking and smoke assailed his nostrils and in the stillness he heard the lap of water on the lakeshore. The varied birdcalls barely entered his consciousness, and the only thing to really intrude on his concentration was the frightened bark of a dog when the Sun Shield was placed in position and caught the sunbeams and flashed its message to the spirits in the sky.

Garaun knelt, transfixed, as were all the others. The ceremony needed no human intrusion. It would hold and mesmerise until the sun set; it would allow the rise and fall of the spirit but would ultimately elevate it to a higher level which would be evidenced in the great glee of all at the feast which would follow and in the activities of the night. Garaun saw his life, each precious moment, each difficult moment, from his first memories to the present point in time. Nanda was part of all of that, directly in youth and indirectly during the years of their estrangement when he so much wanted it to be otherwise. If there was even a slight distraction or if a distraction was possible, it was in the

gleam of the sun on her hair, shield-coloured, and in his mind were the words,
"She deserves it; it is hers," and with the thought ended any regret that he may have had in not insisting on part-guardianship at least. Nor was he sorry either for his approach on Garvok. The boy needed fosterage and he would grow into balanced and accomplished manhood under his tutelage in Aney. Ah! But the Shield! The Sun Shield!

When the sun set and the last beam left the Sun Shield a great cheer was raised but it was strange in that it was a cheer of regret. A cheer of happiness would follow when Nanda signalled, again with the mace, to the perspiration-covered youths that they could now lower the shield. Exhausted but elated, they were now men in the eyes of the tribe. They had come through the test and manhood was their reward, though sometimes it would carry a heavy price not to be considered now. The Sun Shield was returned to its rest-shrine but the reverie lasted for some further moments and the slowly, as if stirring from sleep, the activities of the evening were resumed.

Fires took the place of sun and food was served. Nanda and Garaun sat side by side and enjoyed the good meat and bread and the rich mead which washed it down.
"Do not fear for Garvok, Nanda. He will be taken good care of and when fosterage ends in his seventeenth year, he will return a youth skilled in the arts of the warrior, ready to take on the leadership of his people."

Nanda was thoughtful, hurt that the decision on fosterage had been taken out of her hands, but glad now that Garaun was attempting to console.

"He could have become an accomplished leader here and would have had the benefit of schooling from Becan and the monks. He should not be deprived of that."

"What he will learn at Aney will be more important for him in the years ahead. Later he can seek instruction from the monks."

"Can he visit here for a set period of time each year? You owe that to him and to me."

"I'm sure we can agree on that but only at a time when his other training will not be interfered with. I know that Becan is his father. No! Don't deny it! The abbot is getting feeble and the years ahead could be too long so we will arrange time to visit."

The blush in her cheeks was hidden in the darkness as the fires faded.

"Esk is taking care of Tana and the children," Nanda said, as if defending her relationship with Becan by referring to another, which needed to be formalised.

"She is with child. Who the father is I do not know. A son, and Smet will be reborn. She has told me so herself."

"Esk is a good man and will be a good father. He is the one to whom you should entrust the control of your warriors. He is hungry for revenge for Smet's death. He is the right one to choose."

"He is my choice also and I will seek him soon."

CHAPTER FIFTEEN

"Your mother will miss you, Cahal."
His father was also expressing his own feelings but not in words and Cahal knew by his tone.
"'Tis only right that I should go, Father," he said. "Séamus will be here to help you and take over the farm. It isn't big enough for the two of us. From America I will be able to send home money for dowries for the girls and to improve the place."
"I wonder if Séamus will stay? He will find it hard without you and I know that he will want to join you, but we'll have to take what the Lord sends."

They had moved the calves into the small field of aftergrass on the side of the hill. The cows had been milked and sunset was approaching, the slanting rays turning the still waters of the lake to gold.

"I will miss this place. I will miss you all. But I have great memories to carry with me and the lake will never leave my mind."
They lapsed into silence and later he added,
"In a way it's strange! It's the lake that is sending me away. It gave me the shield."
"Yes!" answered his father, "but it was Old James who got its value for you."
Cahal decided to change the subject.
"This is good grass. You'll have good weanlings for the October Fair in Bruff and good replacement heifers as well. There'll be no fear of the rent!"
But his father refused to be side-tracked.
"I hear you're sweet on the Bresnan girl!"

He waited on an answer and Cahal was struggling for the right words. A blush had risen to his cheeks and he took a step backwards hoping that his father wouldn't notice.
"She's a nice girl...," he heard himself saying and cleared his throat to continue.
"Is she going out to you?" The question came fast.
"I don't know, Father. I didn't ask her. She might have to emigrate being the youngest in the family but she might not go to America."

The conversation more or less ended there, inconclusive. It would be raised again and again finish inconclusively because, while Cahal knew of his feelings towards Mary, he did not know what she might feel towards him, and she was too young to reach such decisions. And yet something kept telling Cahal that, though young, she would decide and let him know before he left home. For all the emotional drain in going away, probably forever, he knew that if Mary promised to join him in a few years time, his leaving would be much easier.
Five swallows landed on the roof of the house.
"They will be going away soon also," his father said softly.
Together they walked towards the house.

That night his father's words kept ringing in his mind.
"I know you're sweet on the Bresnan girl!"
Away and back and again and again! Should he ask her? If he did it would be like a proposal of marriage. It would be a proposal of marriage. He could hear her disdainful scoffing laugh and he cringed at his own folly. Other times the image was of the gentle face smiling wistfully, eyes radiant with love.
"Oh, Cahal, I'm too young! They wouldn't let me go and we haven't any money"

His heart would swell with love and he would promise to send the fare

'...as soon as I reach Boston I will get a job and work and save and you will come to me within a year. Oh Mary, I love you so much.'

Words rarely if ever to be spoken.

He went to bed eventually and his sleep was uneasy. In dreams she came and laughed at his suggestions

'You big fool you! You amadán! Cahal Hayes. I'll not go traipsin' around the world with you. I'll stay here and marry a strong farmer. Tom Dea has an eye for me and he has tons of money, even if he's sixty years of age.'

And with a toss of her auburn hair, head held proudly high, she skipped away into the mists of his dreams.

"Mary! Mary!" he called in his sleep.

"Will you shut up! I can't sleep with the noise you're making. I'll tell her that you are talking to her in your sleep and what if our mother hears you?"

Back to sleep but the images wouldn't go away. He didn't want them to go anyway. The good more than outbalanced the bad.

Now she was atop Carraigcrothera and her voice was harsh and horrid, old and hag-like, croaking out the words of 'The Coolin', cackling between lines, awful to behold, and the next moment it was Mary again lovely and sweet-voiced and his heart beat faster and his hands reached out to her. But just as quickly the hag returned and she leaped from the rock and landed in his bedroom and her tongue was black between toothless gums and cracked lips and her white hair streeled down her back and she came to him, closer and closer, mocking and jeering and he saw her eyes and they were fitted with the coppers of the dead and he screamed into wakefulness, rousing the household in fright from sleep.

"I'm alright, Father. 'Twas just a bad nightmare," as his father came into the room, ghostly in his long night-shirt, with the lighted candle in his hand casting spectral shadows.
"What's wrong with you, boy?"
"He's talking in his sleep about...." But even though Séamus had been woken in terror, his loyalty to his brother stopped him on time.

His father had an understanding of what was happening. He had seen the strain of leaving home on many of his family and friends. Of his own family two of the boys went to America and one to Australia and two of the girls later went to America when their brothers sent for them. He thought of them now but, in the frightened atmosphere, it was the boy and girl who had died of consumption that came to his mind, and it was that fear that he directed at Cahal to console him.
"Your Uncle Nick will be waiting for you in Boston. You have nothing to be afraid of," he said as he tucked in the bedclothes with his free hand and then involuntarily touched Cahal's hair, an action not done since he was a small boy and needed consoling after fall or fight or protection from mother's anger.
"Go to sleep now, son. You are going to the shipping agent in the morning so you need sleep. Good night now! Good night Séamus!"

As he turned to the door the candle threw back his shadow on the wall opposite, a giant figure bending to go out through the low door, but the comfort he had brought to the room remained when he gently closed the door.
"Jaysus Cahal, you were shouting like a madman. You nearly frightened the life out of me. What was wrong with you?"
"Ah, go to sleep. I'll tell you to-morrow." The moon peeped through the window and brought further comfort.

CHAPTER SIXTEEN

The reality was that Smet was dead. Each time Esk passed the place of killing he rebuked himself. 'If only….' But it was useless and yet the image would not go away; the last moments as he held his friend and watched his life-blood flow away. Sometimes when passing this spot Esk spoke to Smet.

"I am doing my best to take care of Tana and your children. She is with child again, my child or yours whichever, but in whom you will return. And I swear that Vullen will pay for your life with his. Trust me, Smet."

He was responding to Nanda's call and was on his way to the fort. In the quiet of the day the drone of the monks in prayer reached his ears. He waved to the youngsters herding the cattle on the hillside. Soon Etan and the others would be called on to do their share, just a few more years. Like the children watching the cattle, the sentries on the strong wall of the fort were watching for enemy activity. Soon they would be strengthened when Garaun's men came from Aney. This was a time when a wise enemy should attack but this weakness was not generally known.

The gate was open and he walked into the lower fort and was greeted firstly by the women and children and then by the smith, Ahbag, as he fashioned a sickle, his son tending the fire.

"May the spirits bless you and your work," Esk called.

"And you too, Esk," was the obvious response and he added, "Nanda is in the house," knowing that it was she that Esk had come to see. Just then Nanda's maidservant called to him and he went to the house. Nanda sat by the fire over which hung a pot from which the smell of cooking meat rose

to scent the air. The open door allowed in plenty of light. Esk bowed slightly in salute.
"You are welcome, Esk. Come and sit by me."

Without being told the maidservant came to the pot carrying two bowls which she filled with soup and meat and passed the first to Nanda and then to Esk. Before withdrawing she also brought freshly baked bread.

They ate in silence for a time and when food was eaten Nanda spoke.
"You know, Esk, that Garaun has agreed to help us in our difficulties. He is being very generous and is not claiming the Sun Shield, but he will spend some time here each year and I will allow him access to it during that time."

Esk nodded in agreement. He had no problem with the arrangement. He and Garaun had always been very good friends and he was well aware of Garaun's concern for his sister's welfare with the burden she carried over the years. He trusted Garaun and knew that his intervention would be positive, indeed was positive. Becan had already made him aware of the contents of Garaun's help-plan, and Nanda knew that also.

She was staring into the fire, staring hard as if fighting to control her feelings when she spoke of Garvok.
"You know what Garaun has offered and you know that I have accepted, am glad to, but the matter of Garvok's fosterage hurts me deeply. I wanted him to grow to manhood here and to become leader when he comes of age. I wanted you and Smet to train him in the skills of warrior and leader. You could do it alone but Garaun will not agree."
Carefully and gently Esk replied.

"We could have done what you say, but Smet's murder has changed that and other things also. You know that your brother has the best interests of the tribe at heart and Garvok fits firmly into those interests. He will be well instructed and well cared for in Aney and will return to us a true warrior and leader of his people. It isn't as if there were hostage implications involved."
"I know! I know! And I should have more sense, but the mother instinct tears at me and dulls my better judgement. This side of my character you will not have seen before, Esk, nor will again, I assure you."

She picked up a stick and poked at the fire and the sparks rose and new flames sputtered from beneath the ashes and Esk picked up some sticks and put them on to counter and complement. Prolonged silence and then..
"I want you to lead. I want you…"

Only he would be allowed to enter. Garvok charged in at speed and straight into Nanda's arms. The impact almost prostrated her but she held on and hugged the little vital body and gained from it. A strength of sorts seemed to come to her from it and she nearly told Esk to go away, that she would lead the tribe until Garvok was ready. When the hugs lessened and the request, more likely demand, for more apples was granted, Esk quietly but firmly admonished, and the implication was that fosterage in Aney was correct and needed.
"Garvok, go out. Esk and I have lots to talk about."

He still clung on, even under Esk's disdain, but she finally pushed him away and with a gentle touch on the cheek pointed him towards the doorway. At this point young Garvok's reticence ceased and he sprinted down the hill, checking and correcting to the uneven slope until he reached bottom and his young friends with whom he would share the apples.

The arrival of the Old Hag further upset the moment of the handing over of the leadership of the warriors to Esk. She seemed to be invisible to the sentries. Nobody had challenged her or announced here arrival. The younger sentries were genuinely afraid of her and if questioned would say that she had the power of invisibility as all knew. She half-bounded into the house, where even the semi-darkness didn't hide her ugly evil visage, her wild staring eyes. Taller than any of the men, gaunt and spectral, she held the adults in dread and never once were the children known to have called her names. How often had they heard 'The Old Hag will take you' and the stories of all the children who were taken by her and never again seen. Nanda felt a shiver of fear as she always did when she saw this woman and no words came to her. Esk's hand automatically reached for his fishing-spear. To him she seemed ageless like his mother had been and the memory slowed his action but he stood poised. Then she spoke and her voice was shrill and her tone was a defiance of the higher social rankings of Nanda and Esk.

"Old Hag has come, not to ask but to give,' and her voice rose and fell in a wave-like monotone. 'She saw Smet in death. It is you who should have died, you, Esk!"

Hearing the chanting of the monks has influenced her tone, Nanda thought, and feared for what she would still say. Esk was standing, his hand still on his spear in warning.

"Say what you will, Old Hag, and leave us," he snapped

"Old Hag knows the spirits and they tell her things, all sorts of things. They show her all sorts of things. She knows things, all sorts of things, all things. She saw Smet die. You did not kill his killer, Esk, you killed the one who tried to kill you. His killer lives. His spirit is not at rest."

Neither Nanda nor Esk wished to argue with her and so they remained silent and she continued.
“Old Hag says that his spirit will not rest because you have taken Tana and he wants her.”
At these words Esk drew his spear and raised it menacingly but Old Hag was uncowed.
“Old Hag is glad that the priest’s son is going to be fostered but Garaun isn’t strong enough to make him the leader needed here. Old Hag sees death and destruction, sees the end of the tribe, sees the offering of the Sun Shield to the spirits of the water, but you will not see that day. The curse, the curse is upon you all,’ and her tone changed on those words to a harsh, awful, blood-chilling scream.
Nanda crouched down and covered her face with her hands.
Esk, with fury flashing in his eyes, leaped across the fire, and with all his might lunged at the Old Hag, driving his spear through her, but she was no longer there. He froze in stunned amazement and more so when he saw blood on the barbs. But the Old Hag wasn’t there and her horrible laugh seemed to linger, as did the smell of her presence. Two young sentries rushed to the door, ashen-faced and perplexed.
“Did you see the Old Hag enter?” Esk demanded
Both answered in the negative and then the older added,
“We saw something strange surrounded in smoke crossing the ramparts a few moments ago, and we heard awful sounds,” his voice quaking in fear.
Esk dismissed them, but not before rebuking them for not being observant all of the time.

Having recovered her composure somewhat Nanda said, “I want you to lead the men, Esk, to take that part of my burden from me.”
“She does need help,” Esk thought, “and I can give it.”

"You can live with Tana but must come here every day and take charge just as Smet did. Our remaining warriors and those coming from Aney will take their orders from you."
"And from whom will I take orders?"
"Mostly decisions will be entirely yours but occasionally you will need to consult with me on matters affecting all our people and with Garaun in matters of raiding and war. You will be well rewarded."
"I will do as you ask, Nanda, at least until I am happy that Smet has been avenged." The words of Old Hag hung like a pall over him.
They took each other's hands and held tight to seal the bonds created. They would carry the burden together, defy the Old Hag, and restore the fortunes of the tribe.

As he left Nanda stood watching from the doorway. She knew Esk was one on whom she could truly depend and, though small in stature, within his strong body was the natural fury to do what was needed.
"Whither my pride?" she thought. "First it was Garaun, now it is Esk," but she wasn't unhappy, rather she was glad that these decisions had been forced upon her. She had every right to be. A new danger was lurking.

CHAPTER SEVENTEEN

"So you're going to the New World, young Hayes!"
"I am, sir. I'm going out to my Uncle Nick."
The questioner was Mr. Thomas Dunne, shipping agent of Bruff, in the County Limerick, proud agent for the White Star Line. Cahal had difficulty removing his gaze from the man's moustache, snow-white but snuff-stained on top and he always had a corner of it in his mouth, which he sucked contentedly between statements. People remarked on this and laughed behind his back and coined nasty nicknames of which Mr. Dunne was happily unaware. He was a jolly man, bald with round ruddy face and an easy laugh. A great fowler, Cahal regularly saw him in the bogs, and indeed he was a frequent visitor to Hayes' where he often left his horse while he went shooting.
"Nicholas has done well for himself out there!"
"He has, sir. He has indeed."
Always dressed in tweeds, he seemed ever ready to drop everything and head off to the hills and bogs.
"A good shot he was too. How long is he gone now? It must be all of ten years."
"A bit more, sir. I can only barely remember him."

Mr. Dunne dipped the pen in the inkwell and finished the document with a flourish, a suck on his moustache and a smile of approval on a job well done. He had asked the questions and been given the required details about Cahal Hayes of Lough Gur, about-to-be emigrant, and they were now on paper. The ticket was also ready.
"Has he any notion of coming home? He always said he would."
"In his letters he says he will, but since grandmother died I'm not sure he really wants to."

Cahal stared at the ticket. Here was the reality. He had paid £8 and the long journey lay ahead. The Sun Shield flashed to his mind, and Old James, forever to be linked, and he asked himself if he would ever again see the old man after his departure, or his mother, father and family for all that, and Mary?

"There are plenty of opportunities in Boston. Will you stay there?"

Cahal nodded in reply, nodded from his trance. Thomas Dunne had handed out many tickets and rarely had anybody jumped for joy. He had seen this reaction often, akin to shock as the reality struck home. He understood.

"God go with you, Cahal Hayes! You're a good lad. Tell your father I'll see him soon."

"Good day, sir, and thank you," Cahal mumbled as he turned and walked out into the street.

The preparations were nearing completion. The Tailor Houlihan had delivered the new suit and when Cahal had tried it on, the tailor admired his handiwork as a true craftsman should, and defended it.

"A bit loose there," his mother remarked, tugging the drooping shoulder.

"Not at all, Ma'am," replied Houlihan. "A growing boy needs room to expand," as he pulled at the shoulder as if to tidy the surplus.

"'Tis you'll be the best-dressed young man in the New World and all the young ladies will be mad after you."

He regretted the words when he saw the frown on Mrs. Hayes' face and as she snapped,

"Don't you be putting notions in the boy's head. Soon enough for that."

But Cahal's thoughts were not with the belles of Boston; they were and would be with his Mary in Lough Gur.

Even though it was Cahal's money it was his father who paid the £2-10-0 to the tailor.
"God increase you," he said in accepting and "God increase you again," when he was handed the glass of whiskey that he quaffed in one quick gulp.
"God take care of you," he said, as he shook Cahal's hand and returned the ten-shilling note to him. A gentle hand on the young man's head and he was away to the pub with money in his pocket. That had been two nights ago.

The galloping horse raised dust from the street and the tall R.I.C. man's shout went unheeded. Cahal heard the rider's retort and it was just as well that the R.I.C. man didn't. The town was quiet enough though the shops were open. Shawled women carried baskets and shopping bags; ill-clad, bare-footed children, who should have been at school, stood listlessly about waiting to beg or to earn a penny holding a flighty horse. The smell of horse and dung was pungent but rested easily on Cahal's well-used-to nostrils. There was a concentration in front of the bank and the removal of the dung would later elicit choice blasphemies from the porter. The strong farmers were in town with money. There had been a fair in Kilfinane on the previous day.

Cahal was barely noticing all of these things. The steps he was taking were his first steps to America. From this point on everything was in that direction. He would sail from Queenstown on the steamer 'Portsalon' on the 26th. of October 1872 and the ten days remaining would be cluttered with expectation and frustration., with thoughts of adventure and homesickness, with anticipation and regret, with some little happiness and much sadness. It would be a time when images of person and place had to be imprinted forever, to give solace when required, to spark ambition, to be his raison d'être, his driving force to success, his triumphant return, the Yank with the dollars. To Mary if she didn't come, and together if she did. Not a moment to spare; so many things to do; friends to meet; messages to carry; memories to store; promises to make; promises to be made to keep; coping with the sorrow his leave-taking was generating. While making sure that everything would be ready for his departure, his mother's face had an added sadness when she sat by the fire staring at the flames to embers, without adding more fuel. She was afraid for Cahal, afraid for him in that far-off land, afraid that ill-luck might follow the Sun Shield, afraid to say goodbye, afraid that she would die without ever seeing her son again, afraid. Her husband's assurance that all would be well and that Cahal would do well, being a good lad and with the help of his uncle, didn't really assure her, because she knew the sense of impending loss that was weighing on her man, the good father. Whatever solace she found came from her beads and often she combined the empty stare with the fingering of the beads, the movements of the lips and sometimes the barely audible whisperings of Paters and Aves. Séamus was also becoming distant, steeling himself for the loss. The sisters were excited at the prospect and the possibility of Cahal sending money for passage and dowry.

As he was leaving the town with its noise and smells, the thought came to mind,
"I don't like these places and what will Boston be like? Ten times worse, no doubt! Still what is is and that's where I am going."
He was passing the last hostelry, 'The Abbey', and the raised voices told him there was trouble brewing. He was nearly knocked over by the charge of men out the door. Quickly a circle was made on the road and the protagonists were taking off their coats, wheeling, shouting abuses and being held back. The 'Can't ye shake hands and stop this

nonsense' attempts were outweighed by the 'Let 'em at it!' The smaller and more aggressive man kept shouting,
" He insulted the Murphys. He won't get away with it!"
Then they were fighting, harmlessly in their slowed drunken action, and then they were wrestling and cursing and rolling on the ground and the shrill noise of the R.I.C. man's whistle pierced the shouting as he laboured up the town. The fight ended abruptly and Cahal moved on.

The fight had raised his spirits somewhat. He crossed the small bridge at the end of the village, passing a few fairly good houses but it was mostly hovels on the Palatine Road. He got many greetings and enquiries about his parents' health and friends in Lough Gur. The news of his departure was as yet unknown to those people but the word would spread before long. At the Pike he turned right onto the old road. Why not stay on the new?
'Stick with the old, Cahal, while you can,' he thought.
It was part of his mood. He thought of the new as representing where he was going. The old was a languishing attempt to clasp his life so far, the totality of it. On the two miles, the two undisturbed miles he wanted to 'see' his life, his twenty-two years. He did his best but his mind-direction was forward and in the jumble of past and future the future gained the upper hand, and before he realised where he was he had exited the old road at the 'Inkbottle' and turned right at the pub. He reached Teampall Nua. The words of the song were in his head; on his lips were prayers for his dead relations and all the dead.

The Poet was striding towards him. Everybody knew that Owen, Mary's brother, had the 'gift', as Mrs. Mack put it. A big man, with tousled hair and close-cropped beard, he wore neither hat nor cap, as if exposure to the elements was a poetic stimulant, but he always carried a walking stick,

which he brandished with a flourish, walking fast, always in a hurry. His poem, 'Teampall Nua', was on everybody's lips now that the schoolmistress had set it to an Old Irish air, and his sister sang it better than anybody else.
They exchanged benedictions. Cahal knew that Owen had been in the States for a short while, 'on Fenian business' it was said. It was further said that it was on the ship on his way to New York that he composed the poem. At least he brought it back with him. The opening lines ran through Cahal's mind...

' Oh, I long to see that churchyard by Lough Gur's romantic shore,
Where the shamrock and the ivy ever bloom....'

"'Tis a good land, Cahal," and he paused, back there again in his mind's eye.
"'Tis to Boston you're going! Make sure you call on the Fitzgeralds. I hear say that Cocky Tom is doing well for himself, and the Moores from the bog are there too."

'..Where the wild dove and the raven like protecting spirits soar,
O'er the green graves of silent Teampall Nua...'

"I will indeed. I expect to be bringing messages to them from home and to many others also. A lot of people are calling to the house."
"I'll give you a letter for Cocky Tom and Michael Hannan."
"Why didn't you stay there, Owen?"
"I was there but my heart was here. Even though I was only away for a short time I knew I could never settle. The lake, the hills... The farm was for me and the parents were getting on and I loved a young woman. Isn't that reason enough?"

..'By that high and hoary gable that defies the wrack of time,
Sleeps O'Connellan, beside the shining wave...'

"Tell me about O'Connellan, Owen."
And the Poet was away.
"Thomas O'Connellan Rua, you mean. The great poet-harper from Cloonymahon in Co. Sligo with the fiery red beard. He also loved this place, and found his final rest here. He had played his very best at the feast that night and sat by the fire to rest with a well-deserved draught. He nodded into sleep. Little did anybody know that it was his eternal sleep until the call went up for the harper to further entertain. But, alas, the harper was dead."
Owen blessed himself, as did Cahal, and a long pause followed.
"And the burial, Owen. The burial!" but Owen hadn't heard.
"The harp remained in the castle and my father heard Miss Bailey play on it. A noble instrument it was, and when the Baileys passed away the proud harp was left in the deserted house and vandalously destroyed...*'cords torn asunder..'*. Oh, the shame of it!"
"The burial, Owen? The burial."

"A gathering befitting the great man. In Teampall Nua, and the likes of the gathering of poets and musicians was never seen before, nor since. Music filled the air, and it wasn't all sad; his great airs were played, poets gave odes of praise and as the remains were interred the banshee cried on Carraig an Iolair (Rock of the Eagle), over there. There was a plentiful supply of drink and the music lasted through the night."

'..Those who loved his Irish melodies enchanting and sublime,
Should raise a wreath of laurels o'er his grave..'

“Yes, Cahal, my song will not allow people to forget and one day he will be properly remembered with his deserved wreath of laurels. Now I must be on my way. There’s a sick cow in Dineen’s.’

“He’s a good man,” Cahal thought and remembered his father’s comment on Owen.
“He’s great with animals but he has more time for other people’s animals than his own. And he’s forever stuck in those aul’ books and writing things down.”
As Owen strode away Cahal’s courage rose and he called after him.
“I’m very fond of Mary, Owen. Do you mind if I write to her?”
The Poet stopped but didn’t turn about.
“If my mother has her way, that one is for the convent.”
The words came heavily to Cahal.

CHAPTER EIGHTEEN

It may have been just a coincidence, but from the day Garvok left for Aney a change came over Becan. Perhaps his health hadn't been very good anyway, and the monk with herbal knowledge concocted many potions, which temporarily gave him some extra strength. Nanda noticed and worried. Their walks became fewer and when they did meet she was nervous that the strain was too much for him. They walked together on the lakeshore for the last time at the onset of winter, but on a day that was warm and clear, the type of day that called people out of doors to glean the last of the sun's weakening rays. The lake was a-glitter, sparkling in the bright sunshine. The seven swans were there, some feeding tails-up. The pen stayed with the cygnets, their last days together as their plumage finally changed to its brilliant adult white from the dirty grey of their gawky stage. The old cob was some distance away, preening his feathers, yet vigilant, on instinctive sentry duty or pondering the separation that was imminent. Becan's wheezing was a distraction, the only distraction, but both were preoccupied with the swans and the wonder of the world, and for a little while Becan seemed to improve and the old vigour returned and the wheezing stopped

"They are slow to part with them this year, but it will happen soon."

He was referring to the fact that the time was almost there when the parent swans would drive their young away, force them to go elsewhere and establish their own territory, take mates and continue their species. The upbringing was now completed. The similarities were not lost on Nanda and she sighed as she said,

"Going away, parting, brings great pain and sorrow."

The words hung in the air. They thought on the swans, but both were really thinking on Garvok, and the fleeting thought came to Nanda's mind that more loss awaited. She felt a cold chill on her spine and her eyes turned to Becan and she knew that he was going also. She quickly dismissed the thought and chided herself angrily. But the seed was planted and taken root and would not go away and it was right and Becan would soon be lost to her also. She wanted to turn to him and beg him not to leave her and her heart felt a weight that should break it in two, but this was not the time. Becan was well and the day was happiness.

"Let us walk here forever," was what she said.

He didn't reply, but stood staring out over the water wistfully imprinting the scene, the beauty, and the peace, which he now sought. Nanda thought that she detected a nod of agreement but as quickly realised that he had not taken her meaning fully.

"Let us walk here forever," she said again.

She watched as he responded, turning towards her, searching for the right words. It was time that he allowed his heart to speak, but the years of disciplined living lined up in protest. His mouth fluttered but the wrong words came forth.

"Forever is not here. It could be here but it is not here for us."

And then he allowed himself a heretical moment when he added,

" The spirits are in the water, under the hills and floating in the air, the spirits of ages past. Would that I could be with them," and he bowed his head and the wheeze returned. Then he was racked with a violent bout of coughing. So severe was it that Nanda feared that he would fall and she put her arms about him and his head rested on her shoulder. Times stood still, constraints were removed, youth was recaptured, bonds restored and they were totally overcome and lost in their oneness. Forever! This was it, and both willed their respective spirits to remain thus. It flashed across Becan's mind that this was the place and the moment to die and he wished that she would join him in death. Together! Forever!

The clatter of strong wings on water broke the spell and changed the moment. Both looked to the water and saw the five cygnets rise and enter formation and wing beats settle into a slow rhythm, swishing through the air. Were they observing a leave-taking? A painless leave-taking? A destined leaving? Could it take place so unemotionally? The cygnets flew to the western margin of the lake and then circled back, banking over their birthplace and parents, honking secret sounds, sounds of farewell. Twice more they circled, at once swooping down and almost landing but rising at the last moment, over the hills and away. The cob and pen moved majestically towards each other, met and with slow dignity turned together towards the setting sun. On the shore the man and woman stood transfixed, held hands and wished themselves swans.

The cold weather came and it took its toll. This year Becan would be included. When she had held him on the day the cygnets left Nanda had smelt death; it had lingered in her nostrils; it had frightened her, shaken her to the core. Becan struggled to rise from his bed, each day fought the good fight, spent most of his time in his own quarters, where on a table lighted by a thick tallow candle, he continued to work on the manuscript. From his days as a young monk his deep interest and skill made the scriptorium his favourite workplace. His prowess was well known and greatly admired. His table was now the scriptorium, an orderly array of inks carefully prepared and quills of swans and goose and vellum of fine quality. He was recording the genealogy of the tribe, Nanda's people, the keepers of the Sun Shield. There he found some ease, lost in the execution of his skill. He struggled to complete, knew that weakness was gaining, but he fought on.

The work was completed, but not by Becan. The chanting of his fellow monks called to him; he tried to work faster, felt a vigour return, saw an end in sight and he rushed towards it. The vigour quickly dissipated into dizziness, the manuscript blurred before his eyes and he fell forward, and head resting on the still-wet ink, blotting the carefully crafted last capital he was to execute. He made a futile effort to rise, imagined that he was in chapel as the evening prayer reached him again. Then silence. He was unconscious when the herbalist monk found him. He would remain in that state for days with very few, and very fleeting moments of coherency.

There are exceptions to every rule. The monastery was a male domain with admittance rarely if ever allowed to a female. It differed in Nanda's case. When the news of Becan's condition was brought to her she immediately went to him and stayed with him until his death some days later. She sat by his austere bedside and took over all aspects of caring for him. He was aware of her presence and he held her hand with little jerks of recognition and understanding. She insisted on a softer pillow and warmer coverings. As she settled his pillow a speck of swan-down rose and she thought on the swans and wished for the days by the shore, days gone and not to return. Day into night and night into day, and still she sat there. At various times some of the monks entered softly, knelt and prayed. They recited the appropriate daily office day in gentle, melodic drone.

Meanwhile the promised help from Garaun had come, and Carraig Aille had been transformed under Esk's direction, and with the additional help of the families, who had transferred from Aney. New houses filled the forts and were also spread down the hillside to the north. The new roofs and palisades bespoke prosperity and strong community. More cattle grazed the hillsides and pastures beyond and raids on them had become very rare indeed. A new era had dawned and Nanda's decision to accept Garaun's offer of help was deemed very wise. Garvok's departure was the only negative in all the happenings. That was, of course, until Becan became ill. The two causes of her concern were closely linked. In a way Becan's illness diverted her attention from Garvok. Perhaps it was her good care and Becan's strong will that prolonged his life over the winter months and into the early spring. Or was it his concern for her when she had remained by his bedside for three days and nights without sleep? At any rate he rallied, but never to regain his old strength. His time was mostly spent in bed and from it he directed the daily routine of the monastery and instructed a young monk on the completion of the manuscript which was so important to him. This was to be his final gift to Nanda.

He managed to rise for an hour or so each evening and spoke of the coming of spring and the improvement it would bring in his health. On Christmas Day he went to the chapel for Mass and prayer, to celebrate the birth of Christ. Afterwards he was exhausted and Nanda chided him when she came on her daily visit. She brought him as a gift, a crude image which the trader had told here was Christ. It was carved in shining jet and he would cherish it and keep it with him, small enough to fit in his hand.

The days lengthened and the first stirrings of awakening life touched the land. The calls of the newly born animals were a source of joy, an unspoken message of continuity. Tana was due to give birth and Esk was anxious, anxious enough to leave the fort and affairs thereof to call and see how she was. He was generally treated with ridicule.
"Esk! Esk! To give life is great wonder. It is not something I fear. Look at the children. They came from me, as this child will."

She placed her hands on her greatly distended stomach and then gently pushed him towards the door. As he returned to the fort her sweet happy voice reached to him with a message that all was well.
"She should sing for Becan," he thought, " that would make him well again."

He was not present when the boy was born. He had gone to Aney, having been assured that that was not going to be the day. He had barely left home when the birth pains began. Tana embraced her knees with her arms and rocked gently and crooned softly. The children had eaten and were playing up and down to the shore. Her eldest daughter sensed that something was happening and stayed very close by. As the pains increased in intensity and frequency, Tana sang louder and her daughter came to her. She still held the same position. Beads of perspiration shone on her forehead.
"The baby is coming," she said. "I want you to help me. He will be called Smet and your father will live again."
"Will I go to the fort for help?" the young girl asked, to which Tana replied with a shake of her head in the midst of the strongest pain yet.

Song, crouch, pain and finally, birth. It was a male child and Tana had enough strength to shake the first breath to his lungs before handing him to Nata with instruc ions on tying the umbilical cord, washing and wrapping. It was done but she had to order her curious siblings out on many occasions. Tana had rested and the baby was given to her. Its hungry mouth found the brimming nipple and Tana admired with pride, smiled in contentment and crooned sounds of love. Time passed.

"The Old Hag is on the carraig!"

The children burst into the house in fear, running to Tana for protection. The atmosphere within changed as the horrible cackling sounds reached their ears. A breeze had risen and was blowing her words away, but all knew that they were not good words and they clung together.

Esk was on his way home, his step rapid, expectation pushing him along. Instinct was sending conflicting signals. When he saw the Old Hag he broke into a fast run, fish-spear aloft and shouting angrily. He passed the house and ascended the hill in full flight.

"Whose child? Whose child?"

Her awful voice reached his ears. Realising that the child had been born he stopped dead in his tracks, looked to the house and then looked up again. The Old Hag was gone. He raced in the door and in the glow of the firelight saw his family safe, saw the new-born babe in Tana's arms, saw her smile of happiness. As he moved closer she said,

"Smet is here Esk. He has come back to us."

It is likely that Becan never knew of the birth of the child, even though Nanda told him, and repeated it many times. On one occasion she thought she felt a tightening of his grip but could not be sure. Death was now very close. She sat by his bedside while the latter stages of his illness came in the form of high fever fluctuating between raging heat and intervals of teeth-chattering cold. When the fever was at its height, words sometimes came. He called to Nanda and she whispered her presence as she bathed his forehead with water from the deepest spring. He spoke words of love, which he had never spoken to her and her heart leaped with joy only to be dashed by the reality of the moment. He spoke words to Garvok and she smiled at the fatherly advice that he would not now give. His own parents and siblings got mention and fellow monks but only fleetingly, returning again and again to Nanda. Sometimes she smiled, sometimes she wept as she whispered words of her love and sometimes in the stillness of the night when she knew that the monks were sleeping she spoke to him of their cherished shared times together; their night of love and the wonder of the life they had created, and she knew that he heard some of these things because he seemed to relax for a time. But the struggle continued and when life eventually left his body and the total calm of death replaced the lost struggle for life, she kissed him tenderly and laid her head on his chest and wept herself to sleep.

Life, and death and death and death! Nanda was next to die and in awful and strange circumstances. Two mournful months had passed since Becan's death and she had spent much time alone. Garvok's absence weighed heavily upon her. Esk was her mainstay but never again did she disclose her feelings to him and this aloofness drew her more and more into herself and people began to wonder. All decisions were now left to Esk. When he called to her to ask or report she invariably asked,

"How is the boy?" and he knew that the question was also a dismissal, at which point he always left, having made comment and wondering why she never once referred to the boy as Smet.

Old Hag murdered lovely Nanda. The circumstances are unclear. Again the sentries failed in their duty. Nobody saw Old Hag enter and certainly nobody saw her leave. Well! Perhaps they did. The hatred that fuelled her action must have been great and grossly evil. Nanda was physically strong and had there been a struggle, she would have fought fiercely for her life. Most likely Old Hag entered the house and killed her while she slept. She then mutilated the body, cutting off hair and breasts and inflicting many wounds. Not a sound was heard. With blood-soaked hands she then removed the Sun Shield and placed it against the bed on which Nanda's scarred remains lay. The doorway faced the east and when the sun rose it struck the Sun Shield. The sentry was dazzled by the light as he opened the gates to allow the cattle out on the hillside. Afraid to enter alone, he called to his fellow sentry and together they entered Nanda's house, fearful of reprimand, calling for permission to enter and receiving no reply. At the doorway they blocked out the sun and darkness blocked out the horrific happenings within. They entered and moved from the doorway and the sun entered once more. The Sun Shield leaped to flame. With horror they saw the dead ravaged body of Nanda. The reflected rays from the Sun Shield caught the lifeless blood-stained body of Old Hag. She was sitting erect, with glazed wild eyes staring at the Sun Shield.

CHAPTER NINETEEN.

On the day before his departure Cahal crossed on to Knockadoon and he walked on the shore reflecting once again on the years of life so far spent. They were happy years and the prospect ahead seemed unattractive by comparison, certainly uncertain. But he knew that the call to go and make his fortune abroad grew with his years also. Many people had left and in increasing numbers since the Famine of the 1840's; some came back proud with the trappings of success, full of tales of opportunities unbounded. They were the lucky ones. Others did not come home, and sometimes the successful ones brought the whispered report of 'the drink' and 'the gutter' and' the inability to cope' in the land of opportunity. Which story will be mine? His mood fluctuated. At once it was the challenge which he longed to involve in, but today the fear of failure surfaced uncomfortably again and again fuelled by the loneliness of leaving home and friends. His mother's face would haunt him. The happiness had left it and he would have preferred to carry a smiling image but the smile had gone since the day he announced his emigration plan. I must change this, he thought, as he climbed the hill. Reaching the top he turned towards the sun and saw the clouds moving in from the southwest heralding rain. An omen? Not at all! Mother, father, family, ships, high seas, sadness, happiness, opportunity, fear of failure, Mary, Mary, Mary....turmoil, and he fought the tears and the beauty he saw about him made him sadder, so he allowed the tears to flow. It was just as well that there was nobody to see or hear. Amid gasps and sobs he spoke to his mother and Mary, at times weeping like a child, at other times roaring in anger and then reverting to soft sobbing. The approaching clouds obscured the remaining sunbeams. The curtain was being drawn down on this part of his life. As soon as he had spoken the words he was released from anger and sorrow, ready for what lay ahead.

"I will succeed! I will come back! My father will be proud! My mother will smile again! Mary will be mine! My lake-home will sustain me! God will be with me!"
His cloud lifted and with lighter step he set out for home.

The mood was sombre but many people called. As the finder of the Sun Shield, Cahal had gained status among a people who were used to finding artefacts of ages past. Especially so since the shield was one of the great finds and had even been mentioned in the newspapers. Mr. Morrison had seen to that and had given a lecture on it to his learned colleagues, which added to his stature very much. The Sun Shield was now in the premises of the Royal Irish Academy in Dublin and it was rumoured, but not reported on, that Mr. Morrison had sold it for a considerable price.

Some older men were sitting around the table in the kitchen when Cahal entered. In an unlikely action they all rose and shook his hand, each giving good wishes for the future. It was an opportune time to refill the whiskey glasses. Cahal was saddened to see his mother just staring at the fire and not involved at all in the conversation. Glasses were raised and Jack Ryan spoke the words,
"Saol buan chugat, a mhic ó! Lámh Dé ar do ghualainn go deo! Go maire tú céad blian agus go bhfeice tú trí ghlún i sláinte agus saibhreas. Bás in Éirinn!"

The clink of glasses and seated again, they reverted to their talk. Cahal sat with them, out of politeness really because he had many things to do.

“We were talking about the shield,” Ned Dwyer said, “and Tom here, was telling us about his uncle finding the gold collar. Tell Cahal about it, Tom.”
Never one not to avail of an opportunity Tom was away.
“’Twas long ago before the bad times, the hot summer of ’35, I think, before the lake was drained and ruined.”
“If the lake hadn’t been drained Cahal would never have found the shield,” Jack interrupted, but Tom was intent on continuing.
“This was a gold collar, the finest ever seen. My uncle was a powerful swimmer then and ‘twas no trouble to him to swim the length of the lake at any time. ‘Twas a Sunday and he decided to have a swim before milking the cows. He swam to the island, Garret Island. He sat for a while in the sun and was just about to go back into the water when he was dazzled by a brightness from under some stones. He had great difficulty because the stones were big, but he was strong and on lifting one huge stone there was the collar. Made of pure gold in the shape of the new moon, the ends fitted with precious stones. He had never seen the like. His hands trembled as he lifted it. You must have felt the same when you found the shield, Cahal?”
He was about to add that, of course, the collar was more valuable but he saw the half-full bottle and his almost empty glass and decided that it was maybe wiser not to say it.
“When the sun flashed on it, he was nearly blinded. What to do? Around his neck he put it and it fitted securely and back into the water with him. He was thinking that it must have belonged to the great Earl Gearoid, or one of the Aul’ Kings that his father spoke about. How proud his father would be, and the Count would surely buy it and they would have plenty of money forever. Halfway across and then three-quarters of the way but then though he swam and swam the shore came no nearer. He was fixed in one place and try as he might he could not get beyond it and the collar began to

feel heavier and heavier. He tried and tried but he was being pulled down. At the very last second he removed the collar and he saw it sinking slowly to the bottom of the lake, glinting in the sunshine. As it settled on the bottom he felt all his strength return and he dived down a few times but could not catch it again. Marking the spot in his mind he swam to shore. He tried many times but never saw it again."

They all nodded in sympathy. On a less solemn occasion comments of ridicule would provoke, but not this time.
"Gold! Gold!" Ned mused, "and there's piles of it in the Money Hole and the Golden Sword is beside the Giant's Grave on the hill yonder…."

The stories would continue for a long while. Cahal wanted to call on Old James. He nodded to his father who acknowledged and he quietly left the kitchen, hardly noticed.

He rubbed the mare's forehead lovingly and put on the winkers. He didn't have a saddle but he was well used to riding bareback and within seconds he was on her back and they were cantering easily along the road. He waved to the people he met on the way, thanked them for their good wishes, but kept on going. He would have stopped had he met Mary and he hoped for that but it did not happen. He looked to the bog and thought of the shield and again when he was passing under Carriage Aille the shield was again in his thoughts. He noticed that the crows were gathering on the tall trees by the lake, raucous cawing filling the air. He rode into the lakefront.
"This could be my last time" he thought, and added, "I hope Mary is here."

But she wasn't, nor was there anybody else around. He sat astride the mare and allowed the image to imprint on his mind, there to remain forever. He thought of fun and swimming on warm summer days; of the great frosts and the merriment and skating and dancing and hurling on the ice; of the stories of Gearoid Iarla, Aine and Fer Fi; of the Green Leprechaun and the fairies within hollow Knockfennel; the chest of gold hidden under the lake which, if only he could find, would mean that he need not leave and go far away. But he had found treasure and it was that which was taking him away, away from home and family, away from Mary

The mare cropped the grass on the roadside as he entered Old James' house having called greeting and hearing the "Tar isteach agus fáilte!"

The old man rose immediately and extended his hand.

"Amárach…Tomorrow…. If I had my youth I would go with you and see the wonders of the great world. It is too late for me but for you there are no limits. Great success awaits you and my prayers will be with you."

He had the book ready and he took it from the table and gently pressed it into Cahal's hand. It was the old man's treasure, his copy of '*Irish Minstrelsy*'. Cahal knew that it was his most cherished possession and tried to refuse.

"No, Mr. Butler! I cannot take it from you."

But it was no use.

"Be my eyes. Read it for me and remember me."

That was it.

Old James then put his hands on Cahal's shoulders and then raised a hand to his head and marked the Sign of the Cross on his forehead and invoked a prayer that Cahal did not understand, but he felt power and strength come into him and he knew that this would be his strength through life.

"God go with you!" And he gently turned him towards the door. The sadness of never again seeing the old man weighed on Cahal but he knew that he now had new strength and blessing and the book. He leaped on the mare's back and galloped home.

Money was scarce but generosity was ever present among the friends and neighbours. Some gave the shilling, the crown, the half-sovereign or sovereign to Cahal personally or to his mother or father for him. Some even gave dollars which they had got from relatives in America intended to pay the rent or the passage for another emigrant or to add to the dowry and make for a stronger marriage. And there were lots of letters. Master Russell had been busy, as had Owen Bresnan, and anybody else who was able to write. He would post the letters when he arrived in Boston or deliver some to those living there, like the Fitzgeralds and the Moores. He had bought his trunk in O'Shaughnessy's in Bruff and, though small, it was quite big enough to carry his extra pieces of clothing and the soda bread and few cooked potatoes and slices of bacon on which his mother insisted to keep up his strength on the long journey. There was also a flitch of bacon for Uncle Nick. He would love that! The trunk was of black leather with brass bands encircling it, fixed in place with studs, and brass mountings kept the handles in place. The clasp was fastened with a sturdy lock for which there were two keys. He was very proud of the trunk. He had once seen a picture of a young lad like himself striding aboard a sailing-ship with a trunk exactly like his on his shoulder and he imagined himself doing the same thing. That was during the better moments and this night was not one of them. Directly under the cover was his book.

The mare whinnied in greeting to the horse tied in the yard. Cahal knew it belonged to Fr. Ryan, the parish priest, who had also come to bid goodbye and give good advice on religious conduct and behaviour in 'pagan' lands. Cahal smiled ruefully. He didn't need advice with the upbringing he had got from his parents, as god-fearing as parents could be. However he was glad that the priest called and he would heed whatever he had to say. He liked the austere tall man for whom he had been a mass-server during his school years. The other men had left when the priest came. This was the mark of respect, but it was done with reluctance and some annoyance because there was still whiskey in the bottle and the stories were good.

"Dé bheath-sa, a bhuachaill," was the priest's greeting and though his Gaelic was scarce Cahal had the reply because it was Fr. Ryan who had taught it to him one day in school.

"Go maire tu i bhfad, a Athair," he said.

"Agus go maire tusa i bhfad freisin."

That was the end of the Gaelic. The priest had stood to greet Cahal and now he sat again. He was also having a glass of whiskey.

"Ah Cahal, we will all miss you. We are losing too many of our good young people to the foreign lands. Our strength goes with them and we are weak without them."

His eyes misted over slightly and he continued,

"The Famine broke our hearts. Young lads like you had to go, whole families had to go. A third of our people fell victim to starvation, death and emigration. We lost in '48 and again in'67. What hope is there for us, James?"

He directed the question to Cahal's father and Cahal felt that he himself no longer counted, that he was one of the many who were gone and removed from Ireland's cause. Not so, he would help from abroad, he wanted his homeland to be free.

"We must get control of our lands, Father. The landlords are breaking our spirit with their excessive rent demands. And

as you so rightly say, our young men and women are being lost to us."
"Our Member of Parliament, Mr. Isaac Butt, believes that Home Rule will solve our problems, but the power of the landlords must also be broken and talk will not achieve that."

Oft discussed but still far from resolution, his words hung in the silence. Cahal heard the tick of the wall-clock, his mother's prized possession, which was part of her marriage portion and had ticked every second of their lives since. The blackened kettle belched boiling water that sizzled in the fire. A hen crossed the threshold and Cahal rose to put it out. The priest rose as well.
"It is time for me to go. I must be home before the dark."

He drained his glass as Cahal took his heavy worsted greatcoat from the peg beside the door. He helped the priest to don the coat and then handed him his gloves and tall-hat. Before taking them Fr. Ryan took a little bottle of holy water from his pocket, sprinkled some on Cahal, who stood with bowed head, and on his mother and father, and as the Latin blessing filled the room, it brought some peace with it.

Out in the yard Cahal held the horse as his father helped the priest onto the mounting-block, asking with concern,
"Are you alright, Father? Would you like Séamus to drive you home in the cart?"
But the priest was now in the saddle and with a "God protect you, young man," was leaving the yard with his great gloved hand raised in farewell. They stood in the yard as the hoof sound changed to trot, to canter and finally faded into the distance.

Young friends came. They stood in the yard in groups of three or four. Each one had the word of farewell, the good word, the word of regret at his going, at their not going. Childhood memories were evoked, the fight in the schoolyard, stealing the apples, the hurling matches. Cahal moved between the groups and the banter was good but for all that there was sadness present, their sadness at losing a friend, his sadness at leaving home and friends.
"My father heard at the fair in Kilteely yesterday that Paddy Ryan from Pallas is going tomorrow also and two girls from Hospital," one of the boys said.

Some had brought him letters to post and little Jimmy Dooley made Cahal take a present of a penknife with a broken blade. Cahal knew that it was because he had saved Jimmy from many a bullying in school.

Down the hill the poet came striding. He barely glanced at the boys in the yard, but to Cahal he said,
"I want to see your father before I give you a letter," and he continued into the house. Mary had not come to say goodbye and Cahal's heart sank. He told himself that he knew all along that she would not come but he had hoped, so very much. Suddenly the whole going-away didn't matter. Whatever wonder or mystery or expectation it held seemed to drain away and become a task, which he must undertake alone.

His friends seemed to sense the change and quietly took their leave, some asking him to write and tell them all about the New World, others barely able to say the words of farewell, choked in emotion for a departing friend. Cahal stood in the doorway and waved to them and then entered the house. The poet was in deep conversation with his father and he knew that it must be serious matter because all

other family members had left the kitchen including his mother.
"I needed to ask your father's permission but it is you, Cahal, who must decide. The content of this letter is of great importance and must reach America safely. Put in the hands of Tom Fitzgerald in Boston it will reach its destination. The Irish Republican Brotherhood in New York has been infiltrated by a spy. Already some of our members have been arrested. It is vital that the spy be identified and this letter will do just that."

Looking to his father Cahal knew that he would approve but also that he would not put him in danger. Owen read the thought and continued,
"Yes! There is some danger involved. If by any chance at all you are caught bearing this letter, you will not be going to the U.S. but you will be going to jail. But there is no reason why anybody should suspect you. Nobody knows that I am in possession of it. Fenian Headquarters asked five of its members to find a trustworthy bearer. Each was given a letter, but I was advised that this might be the genuine one. Will you take it, Cahal, and help your country towards freedom?"

"Yes!" Cahal's answer was firm and he noticed the glint of pride in his father's eye.
"God bless you, Cahal Hayes. We need young men like you. Sew it into the lining of your coat and never leave it out of your sight. Make sure you do not get involved in a fight in which you will have to remove your coat."

The hearty laugh removed all tension as the letter was handed over. Cahal's suit was near the fire and he took the coat and deftly cut the lining and put the letter in place.

Owen took the needle and thread from him and did the sewing himself.

Owen Bresnan, poet and Fenian, rose to go. A slight nod of the head told Cahal that he needed him outside. In the yard he spoke the words Cahal wanted to hear more than any others.
"Mary sends her love and wishes you well on your journey. She says that she would be well pleased if you were to write to her."
Elation! And Owen added, as he strode away, "Maybe the mother won't have her way Maybe she won't become a nun."
"She will not! She will not!" but he did not voice the words.

Returning to the kitchen he found all the family around the fire. It was time for the Rosary and this one was entirely for Cahal and his safety and success. His mother added so many prayers that heaven was bombarded and saints and angels must listen and grant. Afterwards very little was said. Everyone knew what the morning would bring, and dreaded the moment. The fire was slacked down and the mother sprinkled everybody with holy water and the door and windows as well, but carefully avoiding the dog and cat, who slept contentedly by the fire. Sleep did not come easily to anybody that night and Cahal was particularly restless as images of past and future trundled through his mind. But morning came and the new suit was donned and the trunk was waiting by the door. Breakfast was eaten and Séamus brought the pony and cart around. His sisters hugged Cahal amid tears and he had difficulty releasing from their embrace. He would never forget his mother's tears and his own flowed freely also. His father and Séamus were taking him to the station at Knocklong. His journey had begun.

Neighbours stood at doorways and in the fields, stopping from their work to say goodbye.

He could barely see the little figure on Carraig Aille but the voice reached him above the sound of hoof and cart. Séamus stopped without being asked. The words of 'The Coolin' filled the quiet air.

Goodbye to church and school and on over the hill of Knockderk with people still about to wave and wish well. Kilballyowen and on the old road across the hill to Knockainey. Above him was the ruined fort of Garaun, now empty and still. Cahal had never heard of Garaun, nor did he know that the Sun Shield was a common interest for them both, affecting both their lives, though many years apart. A brief visit to widowed aunt and cousins and the low road into Hospital where the bustle of morning was in full swing. Shawled women came from house and hovel with basket and bag going about their shopping for that day. Barefooted and scantily clad children played marbles on the footpath. Séamus was the best in Lough Gur at marbles and on another occasion he would have jumped off and joined in. But not today.

There was very little talking done but as they passed the entrance to the estate on the Knocklong road, his father pointed to the stone balls on top of the gate-piers and said,
"They are there to warn people to stay out. Not so long ago it would be the heads of people who trespassed would be put on the piers."
The he told them that crows had not built their nests there since the hanging of a priest in the Penal times.

The station was an amazing place! The lowing of hungry cattle from the cattle pens was the greeting. For many of them they were on the first leg of a journey which would end in the markets of England. The number of horses and carts and donkeys and carts told of a lot of people leaving on that day. On the platform there were churns of milk awaiting dispatch and firkins of butter, but it was the people who were important. Never had Cahal seen a sight so sad, so much so that his own loneliness abated in the sorrow around him. As the train came into the station its great engine belching smoke amid a screech of brakes, the cries of separation began. The girls were particularly emotional, as were their mothers and their lamentations drowned the engine sound. Knowing that a dignified departure was expected of him, Cahal shook Séamus' hand and then his father's and then, with trunk and ticket, he crossed the footbridge and got on board. He did not look back. Finding a seat by a window he looked towards the Galtees and Slievereagh and he wondered if he would ever see them again. Then he allowed the tears to flow just a little. The shrill sound of the whistle and the train slowly moved out of the station.

First time on a train and soon the sadness was replaced with an excitement, a tingle of adventure, an expectation of discovery, a challenge that must be met and he found himself gearing towards that challenge as the miles slipped by and the stations of Kilmallock, Charleville, Buttevant, Mallow, Mourne Abbey, Rathduff and finally the great city of Cork at Glanmire Station. He smiled when he saw cattle and horses gallop off with tails in the air at the approach of the smoking monster and he was quite unprepared for, and was genuinely frightened, when the train was enveloped in darkness on entering the tunnel as Cork was approached. At each station he again saw the sorrow of emigration but he steeled himself against it, knowing that he would encounter it again and again until they were on board ship and crossing the ocean, and it probably wouldn't end there. There wasn't much delay in Glanmire as another train was waiting to take those who were emigrating to Queenstown. Shy and unsure of himself Cahal hadn't spoken to anyone since leaving Knocklong, but on the train to Queenstown he made his first friends.

Con and Kate Hennessy were brother and sister and Cahal would later find out that they were on their way to New York to join other family members who had emigrated previously and had sent them home part of the passage money. Their home had been in the Glen of Aherlow at the foot of the Galtees. They had got on the train at Emly. Cahal was sitting by the window and a very large woman had sat beside him and was pushing more and more to make room for her much smaller husband and children. Cahal thought that he would suffocate and though he asked politely the woman made no effort to give him more room. Con and Kate were sitting across from him and a trace of smile crossed their faces at his plight. This distracted Cahal. The young girl had been sobbing all along and her brother had been doing his best to console her. The red-rimmed eyes told their story and now a hint of brightness returned, she sniffed and smiled and Cahal saw how pretty she really was. He struggled to free himself and succeeded in standing up. At that moment the train lurched and he fell forward on top of Con and Kate. Before he could apologise the two burst out laughing and he joined in as he picked himself up. Names were exchanged and a friendship began.

All three had been advised to be careful at the ports on both sides of the ocean. When they got off the train at Queenstown they immediately knew why. It seemed as if swarms of young and not so young males were waiting to pounce, offering all kinds of services from carrying luggage to finding the 'best and cheapest' accommodation in town. Some were, of course, honest and genuinely helpful but not all, and many the poor emigrant lost money and luggage before ever getting on board ship and leaving the shores of their native land. Strength in numbers and Cahal and Con ignored all the offers and took good care of Kate at the same time. They would have to find lodgings for the night and the Hennessys had been told to seek out Mrs. Connors who was herself from Galbally. She would take care of them and Con was sure that there would be room for Cahal also.

The whole place was quite amazing to young people who had never seen the like. The hustle and bustle of the harbour town encompassed thousands of activities as ships and boats were loaded and unloaded. Horses and carts and wagons were everywhere, grain, coal, barrels and casks, animal smells of all sorts as cows and pigs were driven along the quay to be loaded into the holds of the bigger ships. When they saw a dark-skinned sailor all three stopped dead, staring in disbelief, but the sailor just smiled at them, well used to being a novelty in this land. But it was the throngs of people that really stunned. Hard to believe that there were so many people on this earth. They saw the sad-faced emigrants, to which group they themselves belonged and they were in the majority. They saw the sailors, the carters, the dockers, the agents, the vendors, the tramps, the paupers, the waifs, horsemen, policemen, cabbies and musicians at corners with ballad-sellers nearby. After a time they were becoming used to this new world, this strange world, the type of world they would have to live in.

"I'd hate to be here by myself," Cahal commented.
"You'd be alright," Kate said gently, "but I'm not so sure about Con and myself."

This remark did not please her protective brother and even though he frowned his displeasure, she knew that he was pleased to have another man along. Time for a rest since the case was getting heavy for Kate but she insisted on carrying it. It was her responsibility and she did not want to make another responsible for the contents, her personal things, her little treasures which would be a little of home in the foreign land. They sat on an upturned boat. High on the hill above the town a huge structure was taking shape.

"It must be a church," Con observed.

A passer-by overheard and said,

"That, young fellow, will be St. Colman's Cathedral, the finest in Ireland when it is completed. Its spire will rise to the sky giving glory to God and its bells will ring across the waters to welcome you when you return."

And he walked dreamily on. The three stared entranced.

"Talking about coming home before we even go," and Kate sobbed softly and Cahal took her hand.

A young sailor lad swaggered past and he too had a trunk on his shoulder, like the boy in the poster that Cahal had seen. When he had gone by, Cahal adjusted his cap to a similar rakish angle, hoisted his trunk and the three of them set out again. His offer to help Kate with her case was refused even though she carried it with difficulty. Before long they reached Mrs. Connors'.

Good food, plenty of talk of home, enquiries about old friends, old places, but the conversation was mostly between the Hennessys and Mrs. Connors. However she had been on a visit one day to Lough Gur and held the memory very dear. It had been a great occasion. The weather had been exceptionally warm all summer. Her father regularly carried butter to the market in Limerick where he was able to get a better price than selling to the buyers who called to the house. They had set out at dawn and her mother, sister and herself had called to a cousin's house beside 'The Swans' at Longfordbridge, there to wait until the father's return from market. While their mothers sat and talked their cousins took the girls across the hills to the lake. Mrs. Connors smiled, eyes soft in recall as she told them of their daring in lifting their skirts high, paddling and splashing in the shallows.

"It took a long time for petticoats and drawers to dry," and she laughed heartily, florid cheeks aglow and large bosom heaving. Before they left in the morning she would hold each of them in turn in embrace to her bosom, giving them comfort and strength. She seemed to be particularly concerned for Kate and gave her lots of advice and warned Con, and Cahal also, to take good care of her.

The 'Portsalon' had entered harbour at dawn. She had come in on the high tide and berthed at the pier beside the station. Coming down the hill the first thing they saw was the two tall masts with sails neatly hitched. Sailors were on the yards checking sheets and halyards, making sure that everything was in order for the long voyage ahead. It was chilling to see them moving so agilely on the ratlines and out along the yards. The smoke was rising higher in the still morning air. This was coming from the one big funnel set aft. Later Cahal would learn that the 'Portsalon' was a British Iron Screw Steamship of 5,064 tons, captained by James Gill. It was a fine ship capable of crossing the Atlantic in fifteen days.

The smell of the sea was strong in their nostrils as they approached the pier, as was the smell of fish. Above the sounds of the morning activity the shrill cries of seagulls were happy and sad.
Con said, "They used come to our garden when my father was ploughing."

“Not much fish there,” was Cahal’s retort, and Kate added, “Didn’t they come a long way? But not as far as we are going.”
“Show your tickets! Show your tickets!”

They did so and passed through the gates.

Cahal had totally forgotten about the letter stitched in his coat until he saw the two policemen inside. Four red-coated soldiers were beside them with rifles at the ready. Clearly they were looking for somebody. Cahal’s blood ran cold and instinctively he took Kate’s arm, a young couple rather than a single lad. A glance showed her surprise but she sensed something and didn’t pull away. They carried on to where the representative of shipping agent James Scott was assembling his embarkees. He would see that their tickets were in order and then the doctor would do a cursory examination. On passing that the gangplank awaited. Cahal sensed that Kate was anxious as she approached the doctor, which distracted him from his own fear. He had reason to fear. Behind them all hell broke loose. The policemen snatched two men from the line of passengers. There was a scuffle of resistance, much shouting and the dull thump of baton on head. The soldiers had moved forward and the second man was dealt the butt of a rifle in the stomach. Then it was over and the two were dragged away, feebly protesting their innocence, as the big policeman shouted,
“Murdering Fenian bastards!”
Christ, but that gangplank was shaky as they boarded the ‘Portsalon’.

The next bout of lamentation came as Roches’ Point was passed and the ship headed for open sea. A mist was coming down over the ocean and most knew that they would not get another glimpse of Ireland. Many had embarked at

Liverpool. They had said their farewells and they were seeing the native land again and now it was fading from sight, possibly for the last time. Bitter tears, but not from everyone. Some were escaping from bad treatment and conditions and they were setting out with hope and very little regret, but the moment brought strain nonetheless. Cahal, Kate and Con stood at the rail on deck and watched in silence.

A good ship! Worth all of the six guineas paid for steerage fare. There was no overcrowding, the allocated bunks were adequate and secure. Many were doubles and in the allocation Cahal and Con were given one to share and Kate was happy to share with a Mayo girl of her own age, Mary Fair, timid and shy and lonely, who had embarked in Liverpool and was all alone. Another friendship! Their bunks were close enough together to be within speaking distance, which was consolation, in the night especially when the strong gales tossed the ship about and her timbers strained and groaned. At that stage, particularly early in the voyage, seasickness was a problem, which added greatly to the misery and fear felt by many. And as the storms passed and the good winds helped to propel the ship faster towards its destination, more time was spent on deck, with the captain's consent.

Mary Fair and Kate Hennessy had many things in common and were also very different in many respects. In appearance Kate was smaller and of stronger build. Mary was taller and thinner and her pale face, framed in a shock of red hair, showed the signs of deprivation, and she told them later that her family was very poor and often had very little food. There was also sickness in the family, which telling surprised Cahal because this was something that people rarely spoke of. She also had difficulty with speech since

Gaelic was still the language of her home. One thing certainly in common, both she and Kate had worked in the houses of their local landlords, sparing whatever possible towards the fare for America. Mary had had no help from anybody. It had been a long struggle to collect her fare. She seldom laughed, but when she did it filled the place with happiness and her face shone at the same time removing all trace of sadness. Then it was a joy to be with her. This did not go unnoticed by Con.

Now there weren't any more seagulls and legs and bodies had adjusted to the rise and fall of the waves and the most times gentle roll of the good ship. The weather was kind also and it seemed that many of the terrible stories told of coffin-ships and wrecks did not apply to the 'Portsalon'. Great was the excitement on the day they first saw the dolphins, spearing their way through the water, fins cleaving the sea like the plough's coulter, racing the ship, agile, playful and wonderful. Mary shrieked with joy and fear when, seeing their tails first, thought they were mermaids. Having lived not too far from the sea, she was very familiar with the tales of fishermen capturing mermaids in nets and the mermaids changing to human form and marrying. Happiness and family, but invariably she escaped back to the sea.
"I'll tell you all about it when we are in bed," Mary told the very curious Kate.

Each day they waited for the dolphins and most days they came and stayed for a brief or long time, nobody could tell why, but there were sighs of sorrow when they swung away from the speeding prow and seemed literally to disappear.

The whale was huge. There was a great cheer when his spout was spotted and everybody rushed to the rail. It was fine while it was a good distance away, but when it came near the cries of fear rose.

"He'll ate us! He'll ate us!" the children screamed, and some adults also.
"He'll not touch you. Just look at him and remember that you are seeing the biggest creature in God's world," and the swarthy sailor added, "Remember the story of Jonah in the whale's belly," which seemed contradictory.
"He has a head on him like Ben Bulben," somebody said, which was lost on most but Mary would be able to tell them about that also in the night.
The sailor had more to say. "When holy Saint Brendan was sailing across the ocean, the tired sailors came upon a sleeping whale and they thought it was an island. You wouldn't blame them, now would you? Look at the size of him."

Cahal interrupted, "The Master told us in school that they lit a fire on the whale's back, and the whale woke up and dived down to the depths and Saint Brendan and his monks were nearly drowned."
Having spurted out this piece of knowledge, Cahal feared that the sailor might be angry, but he wasn't.
"You are quite right, young man. And you have been to school! That's good! You will do well in the New World."

Cahal was pleased and he would seek out the sailor whenever he got the chance.
The whale stayed until sunset, moving with the ship, sometimes close, sometimes a good distance away, diving and appearing again minutes later, sending his spout of water high in the air to the cheers of the watchers. The dolphins didn't come at all that day and night brought a storm.

Down below deck in the confines of steerage the storm is more frightening because one cannot see the approaching wave and steady in anticipation. Fear is contagious and it spreads like wildfire. The captain and crew took very little notice of this particular storm, as a matter of fact they welcomed it since they were running with the wind and making good headway, but the hatches were closed and nobody was allowed on deck. As the ship was carried on the crest of the wave and sank down into the trough, only to rise steeply again, the cries of despair almost kept time with the rise and fall of the ship. Seasickness and foul air, incantations and prayers, the rosary being recited by little groups here and there; fear hung over the place like the few lanterns which swung from the roof giving the only glimmer of light and hope.

Con was sick but Cahal wasn't and if he was afraid he was not going to admit it. He got up from his bunk and, oblivious to the state of the floor, clutched his way across to the girls' bunk. They clung to each other petrified and wailed simultaneously,
"O Cahal, we'll all be drowned."
"We will not indeed," he managed to say as they each caught a hand and held it with a steel grip.
"We'll be alright! Try to sleep!" which he knew would not happen.

He had great difficulty extricating himself when a man nearby called to him,
"Come here, young fellow, and tie me to this pillar and I will play my fiddle and quiet the raging sea."

Cahal did what he was asked and then handed the fiddle to the man who said his name was Dan Murphy from Barraduff in Kerry. Then the music started and it did as he had said it would do. Jigs and reels set feet moving as they lay on their bunks and little by little the cries became silent and the wind and crash of the waves lost their ominous tone, and as people raised themselves on elbows to see the fiddler, soon the clapping began. The swaying ship would not allow them to dance but all knew that they would dance on deck next day. Then Dan Murphy played an angry air, which challenged the storm in its fury, and Cahal knew that it was full of defiance and hatred of the oppressor and floods of memories matched the storm. Next he played a slow, plaintive air, full of pain and heartbreak, which quickly changed the mood and begot woe aplenty. In the quietness, which followed, the storm began to abate. Dan laid down the fiddle to light his pipe, and when the applause ended he called to Cahal,

"Now sing us a song, lad."

How could he refuse! He was haunted by a song of Thomas Davis' that he had learnt from Old James' '*Irish Minstrelsy.*' More sadness, but he sang it anyway and Kate never took her eyes off him. The song was 'Annie Dear.'

'*Our mountain brooks were rushing, Annie dear,*
The autumn eve was flushing, Annie dear;
But brighter was your blushing,
When first, your murmurs hushing,
I told my love outgushing, Annie dear.

Ah! but our hopes were splendid, Annie dear;
How sadly have they ended, Annie, dear;
The ring betwixt us broken,
When our vows of love were spoken,
Of your poor heart was a token, Annie, dear.

The primrose flowers were shining, Annie, dear
When on my breast reclining, Annie, dear,
Began our mí na meala,
And many a month did follow
Of joy - but life is hollow, Annie, dear.

For once, when home returning, Annie, dear,
I found our cottage burning, Annie, dear,
Around it were the yeoman,
Of every ill an omen,
The country's bitter foemen, Annie, dear.

But why arose a morrow, Annie, dear,
Upon that night of sorrow, Annie, dear,
Far better, by thee lying,
Their bayonets defying,
Than live an exile sighing, Annie, dear.'

'O Cahal!' was all Kate said, but the catch in her voice and the tears on her cheeks bespoke emotion, which might never be expressed. He didn't hear the applause and the compliments. Something had happened and he didn't want anything to intrude in it until he could understand his own feelings. He had no idea how much time had elapsed until Dan slapped him on the back with,
'Maith an fear!'

CHAPTER TWENTY

No more storms, just good steady wind filling the white sails which helped the steam-power move the 'Portsalon' swiftly towards the American shore. It was indeed a pleasant voyage and Captain Gill encouraged the passengers to be on deck as often as possible. Also the food was plentiful and tasty, so much so that Cahal had really no use for the provisions insisted on by his mother. It formed a picnic when Cahal remembered them one afternoon and he brought the bread and bacon and potatoes on deck and, joined by Dan Murphy and others, they had their picnic. Mrs. Hayes was given lavish praise for her cooking and baking. In Dan's mind Cahal and Kate were a pair, as was Con and Mary. Cahal felt slightly embarrassed when Dan said,
"I hope Kate is a s good a cook as the mother."

Laughter from the others, a blush from Cahal, a gentle, yet winsome smile from Kate.
He managed to say,
"Stop your nonsense, Dan, and your atein' and give us a tune."

The food had all been eaten by then and the mood was high. Everybody wanted Dan to play, and he did. As the ship surged through the Atlantic waves the sound of Dan's fiddle drowned out the sound of the engines and the deck resounded to the clatter of feet and light-hearted laughter as sets and polkas were danced to exhaustion. Then in the quieter moments Cahal and his book of poems were in great demand, and he read many and sang some. Lady Dufferin's '*The Irish Emigrant*' evoked quiet tears and introspective sadness in the same way as '*Annie Dear*', while '*The*

Wearing of the Green' and '*A Nation Once Again'* were sung with lusty defiance, heads held high.
'*I'm sitting on the stile, Mary....*' And Mary Bresnan was in his mind, and Lough Gur, and home, and he had his own moments of sadness when he read '*The Coolin'* to himself, not wanting to share it with anybody. However each day he was becoming more and more aware of Kate and realising that their mutual attraction was creating a bond in which he was finding contentment. He tried to resist but he knew that he was failing when he began to feel a great emptiness as the ship approached New York, where Kate and Con and Mary were to disembark.

They were two nights out from New York. When the bell was rung to go below for the night Cahal and Kate decided to stay where they were. Earlier they had crawled under some sailcloth to shelter from a shower and the comfort of place and each other's company and the gentle movement of the ship lulled them into easy sleep. On hearing the bell eyes opened and a mutual shaking of heads confirmed shared intentions. They held each other closer and sleep came again.

They awoke as the moon was rising into a sky full of stars whose shimmering images were reflected on the calm ocean. No wind at all so the sailors had earlier lowered and furled the sails. Nobody about and so the world was their own. Love had found them and was leading them willingly towards consummation. It came in many forms. It was clumsy love, tender love, passionate love, violent love, quiet love, frenzied love all converging into tearful love.
"It was wrong of me, Cahal," she sobbed, and as he consoled her the story unfolded.
"I feel clean again, Cahal."
A long pause.

"Tell me, Kate! Tell me what ails you?"
"You will hate me, and love and hate cannot live in the same heart."
"You've done this before? Don't tell me! I don't want to know!"

Cahal's world was falling apart. Love hadn't allowed space for guilt, but Kate's tears and her wanting to disclose something vital to their relationship raised all sorts of fears and imaginings.

"Working in the big house isn't easy. To make things worse a girl has to be able to mind herself from the advances of the male servants. That can be managed but when the lord or one of his family tries to have you it is different. The lord's son came home from the army on sick leave. He had a fever of some sort and had to spend weeks in bed. It was one of my jobs to take his meals to him and as he got better the more he tried to get me into his bed. I kept on refusing and tried to treat it all as a joke and I wouldn't go even though he threatened to sack me. The money came from America to help buy our tickets, Con's and mine, and when we were ready to go I told the housekeeper that I was leaving. The young lord was much better now. I was told to go to the library to collect my wages. It was he who was there. I could see the sneer on his face and I would have run away but he stood between the door and me. He handed me the money, then locked the door and put the key in his pocket. It happened, Cahal. I fought him but he struck me hard and the fight went out of me. I thought he was going to kill me……"
And the tears flowed and Cahal held her and loved her and helpless fury racked him.
"Don't say anymore, Kate. It doesn't matter."

"It does, Cahal. It does. Afterwards when he was exhausted and coughing and gasping for breath because of his illness, he shouted at me,
"Get out, you slut, and take that present with you to America and call the boy Godfrey."

More tears, more anger. The rising breeze stirred the water and wisps of cloud began to draw the curtains on the stars.
"I think that Con suspects. It has happened to many. I could not tell him because he would do something foolish. My parents wouldn't believe, or if they did, would do nothing for fear of eviction, and who could blame them? They know that these things happen to girls who work in the big house. We left home two days later and I met you that day. That was ten days ago now."

Cahal didn't know what to say. His mind was in turmoil. To kill, to console, to kill, to protect, to care for, to kill kill kill!! Mary! Mary! Kate! Kate! Anger prevented tears. Marriage! Marriage! Mary! Mary! Kate! Kate! Kate! They had woken to the lights of moon and stars and now the light of dawn announced a new day, a changed day.
"Between the lights I have found life high and low," thought Cahal, but he did not say so, nor did he release his protective hold on Kate.

"I watched you being squashed by the big woman on the train. When you fell on my lap and we laughed together, Con as well, I knew we could be friends. From that moment I knew what I would do. I wanted you to be the father of my child. I am with child now and you are the father of my child, our child, the child of my love, our love, not of my fear and hatred. It is conceived in love and the memory of what happened is gone from my mind forever."

Con Hennessy and Mary Fair also held each other that night. They were worried about Cahal and Kate but could not search because the hatches were fastened. Con had suspected that Kate had been ill treated, suspicions only. He saw it in her sadness and was glad of the change in her when she was with Cahal. He trusted Cahal, but he used the absence of the two to go across to Mary's bunk where he whispered fears, and in the creaking darkness of the ship's hold, found words of love. They held each other and spoke their words of love, but they would wait for each other until they were in their marriage bed.

The sail-cloth was swept aside; they jumped up in embarrassment as the sailor guffawed in loud laughter.
"Now what will I do with ye, at all? Send ye home to yere mammies and daddies to bate yere bottoms!"
The hatches had been opened and Con and Mary were coming towards them.

Kate waited until the last moment. The 'Portsalon' was entering New York harbour. There was excitement as the city came into view, great excitement, anticipation and trepidation mixed in also. For Cahal there was only loneliness. Kate was going away from him and he did not know what lay ahead, nor what was expected, but he was keenly aware of a responsibility. Nearly everybody was now on deck, the sailors also relieved that the voyage was safely over this far. Boston was only a few days away and there they would have freedom in a welcoming town.

Kate tugged his sleeve and Cahal followed. She stopped quite close to where they had spent the night under the sailcloth.
"Cahal, my heart breaks that we should part…"

He began to splutter a protest but she put a finger to his lips and continued.

"You go on to Boston as you must. Begin your new life there with your uncle. If I give birth I will contact you. If you want me then we can come together. I will always love you and my child will be your child, nobody else's."

"Oh Kate!" was all he could say, choked in the fierce emotion and great practicality of the girl who had laughed her way into his life and then gave him an honour and a burden and a terrible uncertainty. As they held each other in sad embrace the friendly sailor stopped and said,

"What will I do with ye at all, at all?"

He probably didn't know that Kate was leaving at New York and Cahal going on to Boston. Nor did he know of Kate's possible, even probable condition.

The ship berthed and a cheer was raised. Luggage was gathered. Haggard parents herded their children. The engines stopped to a deserved rest. The cries of the docks reached the ears on the decks as sailors put gangplanks into position for disembarking. Ashore there would be regulations to be complied with, medical tests to go through, but the worst was over. For some comfort and prosperity awaited.

"Come with us, Cahal," Con was begging him and Mary was echoing with a repeated nod.

"I must go to Boston to my uncle but we will meet again soon."

"I hope so. I really hope so!" and this time the words were Mary's.

Cahal spoke his words of love to Kate in swift farewell. He bent his head to hide his tears as she set foot on the gangplank. He turned away and as he did he thought he felt

a hand inside his coat. Turning again he bumped into a man about to disembark. The man's hat fell to the deck. As Cahal bent to pick it up, muttering apology through his tears, the man swung at Cahal and connected. The next moment they were rolling on the deck and as sailors pulled them apart. Cahal's coat was ripped and Tom Fitzgerald's letter from Owen Bresnan became visible and was snatched by a young sailor. As he attempted to leave, the friendly sailor tightly grasped his wrist.
"For me, from my poor old mother, God bless her!"

Further pressure, lessening resistance and the letter changed hands again. Cahal was ready to fight but something told him that there was now no need.
"The captain will want to know what my poor mother has to say."

The wink prevented Cahal from springing forward. The incident had passed. People drifted away.

"I'll keep this for you until we reach Boston. It is safer this way. I know! You can trust me."
Lowering his voice he added,
"He was a British agent and has been watching you since you embarked."
Cahal was aghast. So there was real danger.
"But, of course, you didn't notice anything. You had only eyes for one person, and no blame to you."
Cahal felt the colour rising in his cheeks.
"So he knew about the letter?"
"He did, but he needed to be sure. That is why he tore your coat. He also knew that he was being watched by me."
"Owen Bresnan said that there were four or five others carrying letters also."

"Indeed! One of the men arrested at Queenstown was carrying one, but not the real one."
Cahal asked if he was carrying the real one but didn't get a reply. He then asked,
"Will they be waiting for me in Boston?"
"Our friend will not get the chance to tell anybody. We have a welcoming party waiting for him," and he turned and walked away.

Kate! From the rail he searched the crowd below but he did not see her.
Lost! Gone! Gone?

How many days? It didn't and doesn't matter. The voyage had become a voyage of life and Cahal was now left alone, drained, distraught, complicated and afraid in more ways than one. Kate had become his all-encompassing concern and yet she had remained detached to the point that he sometimes questioned her declared love. He didn't question his own. He raged at the treatment meted to her at home and vowed revenge. Father of a child! The turmoil of knowing and not knowing, the longing, the waiting, the need! Was it love that this young country boy had found, was imposed on him? This strangeness filled his being and upset his direction! Kate, I miss you so much!

'Portsalon' berthed in Boston and Cahal set foot on the land that would hold him for the remainder of his life. All the passengers were passed healthy by the doctor and official who came on board; disembarkation was swift. He never knew him other then 'the friendly sailor', nor did he ask when the letter was returned to him as he approached the gangplank on his first steps into the new country.
"You're a good garsún. Go maire tú ibhfad!"

....

"Thank you! You knew all the time. Go raibh maith agat!" No more than a touch on the shoulder, which carried the greatest benediction for success and the two parted. Their lives had crossed, had touched special moments, and had focussed on helping to solve the problems of their native land. Done!

Uncle Nick hugged him with a strength that encompassed all his relatives in Ireland.

"Ah, 'tis great to see you, boy!"
Cahal gasped for breath on his release and spoke greetings from all at home, which brought tears from Nick and rebuke from his American wife. They had their four children with them, the cousins, three girls and a boy. The girls were ten, eight and six and the three-year-old boy snuggled close to his mother and chose to ignore his Irish cousin.

"The house is only a short distance, so we'll walk. I'll carry your trunk, Cahal."
"No need, Uncle Nick, thank you," and he hoisted it onto his shoulder, sailor style. "There's a nice flitch of bacon inside for you."

Nick lifted his youngest daughter on his back and they set off. Nick asked a hundred questions, enquired about a hundred people and shed a hundred tears before they reached the house. While keeping up the conversation, Cahal was being bombarded by the environment in which he now found himself.

The North End was now home to thousands of Irish many of whom lived in squalor, which Cahal was quick to notice. In conversation with Nick he heard the paradox of the new landlords; these were their own countrymen who now behaved very often in worse fashion than the landlords at home. Houses were divided and subdivided to maximise the income irrespective of the conditions under which the tenants lived. How easy to forget! The seed of inhumanity is easily stirred to life!

The Hayes family lived in Hanover, doors away from Thomas Fitzgerald's. Mr. Fitzgerald to his face, but Cocky Tom behind his back was doing very well for himself. His partnership with his younger brother, James, had led to prosperity for both. Their grocery trade flourished and the premises served as a saloon by night. His family had spacious living quarters and the rest of the house was divided and rented. He had already bought two other houses and these were the overcrowded homes of many. It was young John Francis who greeted them when they called to 235 Hanover, his frail physique overshadowed by his expansive manner, his warmth and the glint of roguery in his eyes. Barely fourteen and already unusual in having education, confidence and a licence to sell newspapers and having the best stand in Boston at the corner of Park St. and the Common. Cahal immediately knew that this meeting could bring friendship.
"Bring them in, John Francis! Bring them in!"

Mrs. Rosanna Fitzgerald was already clearing the table, to lay it again to give tea to the visitors. The signs of big family and little help were evident in the disarray, and there was a baby in the cot, a baby crawling, a baby just walking, some older, some at school, others in the streets and she was pregnant again.

They were sitting at table being entertained by John Francis, who had helped his mother by making the tea and cutting the bread, talking all the time while he did so. Cahal rose when Tom Fitzgerald entered. He saw a broad strong man and noticed the slight cast in his eye, which gave the nickname 'Cocky Tom'.

"The Fenian sympathiser is in my house and I'm not sure that I like that."
Cahal froze but the smile put him quickly at ease. Nick placed a hand on his shoulder and said,
"He has a letter for you from Owen Bresnan of Lough Gur. Give it to him, Cahal."
Which he did, and as the envelope was being opened the question was asked as to how the people at home were. As if the answer was already known and disposed of in the memory of misery remembered, Cahal's expected refocusing on home and chance to bear good news was quickly altered when an angry Tom Fitzgerald blurted,
'What's this? What's this?' holding up an empty sheet of paper and showing it back and front.

Cahal's heart sank. So the 'friendly sailor' had not been a friend at all.
"Was this letter ever out of your possession?" Uncle Nick was asking in embarrassment and concern.

He felt hurt and annoyed as he told them briefly of the fight and the 'friendly sailor', his taking of the letter and returning it on the gangplank in Boston harbour.
James Fitzgerald had come in and heard the story. Younger than Tom and dapper in dress, he said,
"This could cause trouble for us all, and for the cause. It is better that he be taken to O'Reilly."
It was agreed for the following evening.

The question of home was returned to. The years away had dulled the memories or they had been stored in a place to

which the key had been consciously lost. But there were comments and questions.
"I remember your father," Tom said, and added, "how old is he now?"
He didn't wait for an answer because he and James took up the home theme, led by James.
"Who did we know? Who can we remember?"
To which Tom replied, " The Hayes', the Moores, the Hannans and, of course, old James Butler. He must be long dead now."

"He is not! He is very well!" from Cahal, as pangs of loneliness filled him almost to tears. John Francis rescued him. He beckoned him to the other side of the room, where they could talk while the other three revisited Lough Gur and Bruff, drank too much and were at once condemning and praising the homeland, the auld country, the old sod. Drink and tears are soulmates!

"When I finish with the papers in the morning I'll call to Mr. Hayes' for you, or if you like, you can come to my newspaper stand whenever you want. Your uncle will tell you the way," and Cahal knew that that was exactly what he would do.
"Time for you to be in bed, Johnny," his father called, "you have to be up before any of us."
To Cahal he said, "You're very welcome here, young fellow, and if O'Reilly agrees we will find work for you. This letter business must be sorted out first."

A tired Rosanna was still working as they left the house. She smiled and said,
"Take good care of him, Nick!"

They hadn't far to walk to Nick's home and Cahal had to steady his uncle on occasions and the talk of home would last into the early hours.

The wonder of it all! Crossing Boston Common the golden dome of State House was stunning. And so many people! Mostly so well dressed, and horses and carriages and hackney cabs and nursemaids pushing perambulators. He knew that many of the girls were from Ireland but he was too shy to speak to them. Kate! Was she doing the same thing in New York now?

He stood and watched his younger friend, now dealing mostly with the latecomers, the older folk. The banter was good and Johnny, yes! He would call him 'Johnny,' was so pleasant and kind to every one of them.
"All gone!" Johnny beamed. "Now we will go for our walk, but first we must go to Mrs. Molloy for the tea."
And so began memorable and pleasant hours for the young country boy in the big city.

Mrs. Molloy plied them with as much bread and butter as they could eat. She teased Johnny about the girls and the talk between them was full of laughter. He was well able for her and Cahal was thrilled to be in his company. This was a vital cheerful person, with a silver tongue, as Old James would say.

They set off and Johnny was telling him all about the American War of Independence which was fought and won over a hundred years before.
"If we could only do the same at home," thought Cahal.
As they passed 'The Green Dragon' he said

“In there they hatched the plans.’ And the names poured out ‘Adams, Hancock, Revere….’ And then they came to Paul Revere’s house.

Johnny was away into the recitation of Longfellow’s poem:
‘Listen, my children, and you shall hear,
Of the midnight ride of Paul Revere;
On the eighteenth of April in ’75
Hardly a man is now alive,
Who remembers that famous day and year…..’

At St. Stephen’s Church,
“This is our church. Designed by the fellow with the strange name of Bulfinch, it was sold to us around 1860 and we were all baptised here and had Communion and some had Confirmation. This is our church and we are proud of it. I served Mass here but I’m getting too big now” and he led the laugh himself because ‘big’ didn’t as yet apply to him.
They walked on; Johnny was talking non-stop. They reached the Old North Church. More Longfellow,

‘Hang a lantern aloft on the Old North Church as a signal light,
One if by land and two if by sea and I on the opposite shore will be
Ready to ride and spread the alarm………’

Johnny’s enthusiastic telling was totally captivating.

Coming back into Boston Common Cahal heard the word ‘muckers’ for the first time. Johnny’s immediate show of aggression was enough to move the swanky boys to run and fast.

"That's what they call us," he said, and changing the subject added,
"The river is called after you. No longer the Charles, henceforth the Cahal River."

What a day! They arrived home and the food was ready and much appreciated. The baby cries didn't upset appetites at all.

James Boyle O'Reilly was now an influential man in Boston; he was part owner and editor of the 'Boston Pilot.' Born in Dowth in Co. Meath, he had worked in newspapers from a young age; had been in the British Army, was a member of the Fenian Brotherhood; was captured and transported to Van Diemen's Land and had escaped to America. He was also an acclaimed poet. The stuff of heroes and Cahal knew this as he entered the room in Staniford St. The two men were seated in front of the good fire, content with drink and cigar. If Uncle Nick hadn't described O'Reilly Cahal wouldn't have known the men apart. Introductions were deemed unnecessary for the young. He would discover that the companion was Robert Dwyer Joyce, medical doctor and composer of '*The Boys of Wexford*' and many other fine poems. That poem was in his '*Irish Minstrelsy*.' Joyce's brother, Patrick, was doing great work on many fronts at home and especially in the training of teachers in Marlborough St. in Dublin. Cahal was an interruption and was treated as such, neither being asked to sit nor offered a drink.

"You don't have to worry about the letter. You lost it to good hands. It carried important information, information that will save lives."

"Well done, young man," Joyce interjected, and absently asked if Cahal knew Glenisheen and its people, but Cahal did not.
"You are now a Fenian suspect and in danger," O'Reilly was saying.
"That man who attacked you is an English spy. He wanted you to be arrested because he knew you were carrying a message. The sailor, I believe you referred to him as the 'friendly sailor', and it is only thus you shall know him, belongs to the Brotherhood. He worked on the 'Portsalon' to make sure that you travelled safely."
Cahal was amazed. The 'friendly sailor' seemed to be always about.
"If Kate only knew."
"The letter wasn't from Owen Bresnan to Tom Fitzgerald. It was from the Head Centre to me. We have found that this is the best method of getting safe delivery. There were others looking out for you also."

He wasn't told anymore. He wondered if Con was involved? Or the fiddler from Barraduff?

Joyce was now reading and sipping a drink. This was really none of his business, from the organisation end at least. His poetry would incite young men to fight. He had helped to immortalise the men of 1798 with '*The Boys of Wexford*' *….'o break in twain the foeman's chain, and free our native land…* 'O'Reilly was deep in thought, and in the silence Cahal recalled one of O'Reilly's great poems also, '*My Native Land.*'…

'My first dear land, all dearer for thy grief!
My land that has no peer in all the sea….'

He was quickly shocked back into reality when O'Reilly said,
"I don't see any other way! Your presence in Boston can cause trouble. Men seen speaking to you will become suspects, even if they are not already. There's only one solution."

Johnny was waiting for him when he came out and he saw the surprise and annoyance on his face.
"They won't let me stay here, Johnny. They say that I would cause troubles for others. I am to go to San Francisco where there is a good job waiting for me with a Mr. Talbot. I wasn't given any choice. I have another bloody letter now but this one doesn't contain any secrets. 'A letter of introduction' O'Reilly called it."
"I'll be sorry to see you go and so will my parents and Mr. Hayes and his family. When are you leaving?"
"In the morning on the train. Ticket and all."

The two young 'muckers' sat on a bench on Boston Common. The setting sun created rainbows among the spurting waters of the Brewer Fountain. Johnny listened intently as Cahal told him about Kate.

"I hope you can understand, Johnny. I have to tell somebody and I have nobody else. The letter will come to Uncle Nick's. It is better that he doesn't know my address in San Francisco, at least for the present, but as soon as I have one I will write to you. I will ask him to give the letter to you and you will forward it to me."
Johnny nodded agreement and they shook hands firmly as the sun went down.

CHAPTER TWENTY ONE

Nefa Rua, Garaun's youngest daughter, was Garvok's best friend. They loved each other, delighted in each other's company, wanted only each other, but the blood laws would not allow their love to culminate in life together.

"'Tis only because I look so like your mother, Nanda," she would snap at Garvok when he looked at her with undisguised love and they felt sorry for their position. Their births imposed responsibilities, which they often considered, but never could, shirk. Sacrifice built on generations of sacrifice, or was it the just demand of born position?

After Nanda's death young fury was exemplified in Garvok's tear-filled reclusiveness and rash unbridled attacks on sentries who had been warned to keep him within the confines of the fort. Reluctantly Garaun had him bound, afraid of the damage he would do to himself or others. Yet he admired the potential for battle-fury which he knew would be essential when, as a trained warrior, he would return to Carraig Aille and lead his tribe. Were it not for Nefa Rua that day might never have come. It was she who wove the spell of his salvation. She began in the simplest fashion. She removed his bonds without the permission of her father and leader. She did it without demanding a promise of behaviour. She imposed her young will on his disturbed state. She shone brightness into the gloom of his sorrow and he clutched at the new presence in his despair and Nefa Rua saved him and made him, but could not have him. The world can be cruel, is cruel, but it needs to place the heavy burden on some of its children for its perpetuity. Nefa Rua and Garvok were two such!

It isn't that they were always together because each had particular personal pursuits to engage in, but when time allowed they were regularly together. If their personalities had not been so strong they would have been ridiculed by their peers. That didn't happen because of the respect they merited. Nefa Rua was different from the other girls. She crossed the line between household pursuits and manly pursuits. She handled sword and spear with dexterity, wrestled, rode a horse and played the game of hurling almost as well as Garvok himself. Almost! Perhaps better, but her female guile controlled any superiority. Just a little less than equal! Hers was beauty and grace, and so agile was she that she was the best dancer by far in the tribe. This young woman of so many fine physical attributes also had gentleness, concern for others, a love of learning but,
"I wish I could sing," she would say, because she could not, even though she excelled on the harp.
Garvok would mock, "The fairies stole it when you were a baby. We must find a way to get them to return it. We'll go across the hills to the cave and ask them for it."

A joke and excuse to be alone and they would happily set off, often hand in hand, to the summit of the eastern hill where the burial mound of Aine allows her a benign observance of the activities of her people. Being the chieftain's daughter meant that Nefa Rua attended school also and their teacher, who was file (poet) and seanchaí (storyteller), told them the epic tales of the locality.

"From this hill the great Cúchulainn was pointed out the surrounding hills and mountains by his charioteer, Laeg. Fionn and the Fianna frequented the hill regularly. It was to here that the Giolla Deachair came to offer his services for a year and a day and punished the Fianna when they were refused. Fourteen of those noble warriors jumped on the great ugly horse's back and became firmly stuck there. As it galloped away Conán caught the tail and he was dragged away also. They were returned only when Fionn and the Giolla reached agreement. And it was also from here that the white fawn lead Fionn to the lake where the lovely maiden wept for her lost ring, fallen in the water. Gallant Fionn dived in to recover and was turned into an old old man. He had great difficulty convincing the Fianna who he was, and were it not for his tooth of wisdom, he would have remained in aged state. He told them where the witches lived and thus the spell was broken though his hair remained white ever after."

Garvok particularly loved these stories and Fionn, Oisín and Diarmuid were his great heroes. Nefa Rua preferred the stories about Áine. It was in her honour that the Bel fires were lighted to greet high summer and it was well known that she was always in attendance at the celebration, as were her spirit subjects. Jumping over those fires was great fun and the best and bravest were Nefa Rua and Garvok. Only the women took the piece of burnt stick and kept it in a pouch suspended round their necks to keep them from harm. It was a wild occasion indeed when all the cattle were brought from the fields to be herded around the fires; their fear and bellowing when their backs were scorched with burning embers. When all this was done celebration of feasting and dancing lasted until dawn. A happy time indeed!

"She carried the big rocks down to the river in her apron," Nefa Rua would say, proud of the female accomplishment.
"She did not indeed. Only a giant could move those. I bet it was Fionn who did it."
The disagreement would dissolve into laughter after some slapping and pushing and added banter.

They were on the hilltop on the last evening before Garvok's return to Carraig Aille and Lough Gur. Theirs would not be an emotional parting. They had promised to visit each other often. They would continue to meet; their friendship was well-sealed, well-tested, well-tempered. As they approached the summit Nefa Rua was thrilled to find the first Meadow Sweet of the year in bloom.
"Áine's flower! Let it be a good omen!" she prayed.

They spoke little. They just sat side by side, shoulders touching, holding hands, her head sometimes on Garvok's shoulder. They asked blessing from the setting sun, on their lives together and apart, hands now clasped tightly. They walked and stopped at Leaba an Triúr, where the great warriors were buried. They clasped hands again as they had often done there and pledged together,
"We will seek for honour such as was on them bestowed."

Garvok's fosterage was over. Soon he would lead his people, but for the present he would study under Esk's good leadership. Destiny held strange store for Nefa Rua, but she would be equal to it. Garvok returned home on the next day.

CHAPTER TWENTY TWO.

He had travelled far to Boston. He thought he was at journey's end but, in fact, he was but halfway to this final destination. The second half was covered much faster as the train steamed across the United States, passing through great cities, vast cornlands and the prairies where the cattle roamed. Seeing a herd of buffalo one day was a memorable moment. He heard tales of savage Indians and thought,

"It's their land that's being taken from them, as was done to us at home."

Cowboys and white-faced, long-horned cattle; train robbers; but he didn't encounter any. Across the great plains and up into the Rocky Mountains; through the pass and first glimpse of the Pacific Ocean and he knew that he had travelled far. Yet part of one always stays behind.

The letter of introduction to Mr. Talbot assured him of a job and a well-paid one at that. San Francisco was a growing thriving city. The gold rush of 1849 brought thousands in search of fortunes. Many of those who succeeded chose to settle in San Francisco and their money set up businesses and built fine houses, some were like those Cathal had seen on Beacon Hill in Boston. The coming of the railway was the key to an era of prosperity. James C. Talbot didn't 'strike it rich' but he made enough to set up a hardware business that was now 'striking it rich.' A native of County Wexford, his grandfather had died at Vinegar Hill in 1798. He was a strong supporter of the Young Irelanders and the Fenians. His staff was Irish in the main, some of whom had been transported to Van Diemen's Land after 1848, served their sentences and then crossed the Pacific to California. Others, one such being John Kenneally, had escaped without completing sentence, as had Boyle O'Reilly. It was John

Kenneally, a kind but severe man, who met Cahal Hayes when he disembarked from the Union Pacific, lonely and unsure and now very far from home. It was with the Kenneallys that he would live in Xavier St. in San Francisco where he would be mothered by Mrs. Kenneally whose two children had died in infancy. John Kenneally, or Mr. Kenneally as Cahal would always call him, took him under his wing in a detached form of adoption, patriotism and paternalism in even mix. Working at Talbot's was not easy, but Cahal was well able for the labour of the yard where he worked at loading carts with timbers for building the expanding city, and unloading consignments from the port or the forest. He enjoyed his work, made friends and little by little the pains of loss of Kate and home abated somewhat.

"You're a good lad," John Kenneally said to him one day when he had been working there for over a year.
"Mr. Talbot is keeping an eye on you and he is pleased. I told him that you are able to read and write and he wants you to work in the shop. Your pay will be better. Will you do it?"
Cahal couldn't refuse. This was an excellent offer.
"Tell him I will, Mr. Kenneally."
"When you know the shop you will go to the office and after that you will become a manager and that's where wealth begins."

Mr. Kenneally was at home before him and had told Mrs. Kenneally, who had a special meal prepared to celebrate. Afterwards Mr. Kenneally offered Cahal a small drop of whiskey and they raised their glasses. It was Cahal's first drink.
"Today is your lucky day, Cahal, you got two letters also," said Mrs. Kenneally, handing them to him. One was from Boston, the other from Lough Gur. His heart raced. He

finally excused himself and walked to the park. He sat on a seat beside the pond. At the far side a stork stood in the shallows statue-still. What news did these letters carry? He looked at the envelopes and felt fear. He recognised Johnny's handwriting on the one from Boston, He wasn't sure of the writing on the other. He opened the Boston one. Inside was a short note from Johnny and another sealed envelope. It bore a New York stamp. It wasn't Kate's writing. His hands shook as he opened it.

No address. No date.
It read:
Dear Cahal,

I hope this letter finds you well as I am well myself, thank God. As you can see I have difficulty in writing and please excuse my spelling also. I also have difficulty with the news I send you.
Cahal! Kate is dead! God, I thought I could never write those words. My heart breaks and I know that yours is now breaking as well.
(Mary's handwriting).
It's better that I tell you, Cahal. Con is not able just now.
We were made welcome in New York by Con's and Kate's relations and I was so happy because I had nobody to go to. Even though we had only known each other for a short time Con and I knew that we were for each other. We knew that since the night you and Kate stayed on deck. As soon as we could afford our own place, we would marry. Jobs were waiting for Con and Kate; Con in construction, as they call it here, and Kate as a nurse-maid to an Irish family. You will understand later why I don't give their names. I got a job as a seamstress in a clothing factory. It was hard work and the hours were long, but we were all glad to have work to do. Con boarded with one family of his relatives, I with another

nearby. We met every day and we saw Kate every Sunday. As soon as Con had enough money he proposed to me. He didn't need to buy a ring because I had my grandmother's Claddagh ring that I had kept hidden but now wore proudly with the heart pointing in. It is now on my left hand because we are married. Kate was my bridesmaid. We have our own little apartment and Con is doing well and we are very happy.

Kate was happy also, but she missed you and was always talking about you whenever she got the chance. You had given her the words of 'Annie Dear' and she often sang it and always said that it was your song. The family was very good to her and she loved the children, a boy of four, a girl of two and the baby. She took them to the park every morning where, she told me, she met many girls from Ireland, not all as well treated as she was. Soon she knew that she was pregnant.

"I am carrying Cahal's child. I am so happy," she would say over and over again.
She waited as long as possible before telling her employers. They were sympathetic and helpful and she stayed with them until she was in her ninth month. The priest then arranged that she should go into a convent to give birth. She made it very clear that her child was not for adoption. I want you to know, Cahal, that all of those people were very good to Kate and helped her in every way possible.
"When our baby is born I will contact Cahal. He will be so proud," she would say.
It wasn't to be like that, God help us. For four days she was in labour and suffered great pain, but bore it all, happy that her child would soon be born. The doctor was worried too and spent long hours with her doing what he could. Con and myself were there when the baby was born. She is

beautiful, Cahal! The doctor said that he couldn't save Kate. Oh, Cahal, I am blinded with tears. I cannot write....
(change of handwriting)
Con again, Cahal. She held her baby and called your name. She wanted to live, to be with her child, to be with you, but she knew that her life was slipping away. Moments before she died she whispered,
"Tell Cahal that God didn't allow our love, didn't allow us to be together and watch our little girl grow. Con, I want Mary and you to keep her, to raise her as your own. I don't want Cahal to be responsible for her without me. It is better that he be free to live his own life. Tell him that he cannot refuse my last wishes. Tell him that I love him and our little daughter."
Those were her last words. She kissed the baby and a tear ran down her cheek and she died. I cannot write anymore...
(change of writing)
This is Mary. We are doing as she asked, Cahal. The baby is three months old. We love her very much. Everybody thinks that she is our child and in a way she is. She looks like Kate and that's her name, Kate Hennessy. She will have a brother or a sister in about six months time, with the help of God.

I hope that you are not angry with us. We are doing as she asked. We have decided not to give you our address because you might come here if you had it. I know you could find us if you wanted but I ask you, Cahal, not to come, at least for a few years. We will take good care of Kate. Oh, Cahal, I am so sad that things turned out like this.

With all our love,
Mary, Con and Kate.

Oh God! Oh God! A heartbroken young man sat on that park bench and wept uncontrollably.

It was days later before he read the second letter. It was from Mary Bresnan. The address was there: Lough Gur, Holycross, Bruff, Kilmallock, Co. Limerick, and it read:

Dear Cahal Hayes,

I got your letter. You have travelled a long way and I'm sure that Lough Gur and myself are as far away from your mind as you are from here. Everybody is talking about the journey you've made. We are all well and all your friends send their best wishes. Poor Séamus is still sad without you. He knows now that he will not join you. Your father really needs him.

Nothing much happening here as usual, but you will be sad to hear that your friend, Old James, died last week. He was found dead in his chair with your letter in his hand. His dog created ructions and the neighbours were with him quickly. He was buried in Teampall Nua. Lord have mercy on him.

There was no trace of affection in your letter so this news will not upset you. I am going to be a nun in the convent in Bruff. I know my mother always wanted to put me away in someplace safe but it is my own decision. I know that God is calling me. By the time you get this letter I will be in the convent with my lovely hair chopped off. I hate that. I will pray for you everyday. No doubt you will marry a Yank and have a flock of children. God bless you and her whoever she will be.

Whenever I sing 'The Coolin' I think of you. In a strange way it is for you. From now on I will only be able to sing it in my mind. Convent rules are strict. Owen wrote a new song called 'The Maid of Lough Gur.' This is the first verse:

'I know a maiden fair and young, but I can't tell you her name;
She lives down by sweet Lough Gur's side, that noted place of fame,
Where Desmond's castles towering high, where knights and chiefs did reside;
I'd forever stray with that maid so gay, down by sweet Lough Gur's side.'

There are five or six more verses in it but I haven't time to write them. He says the song is for me but I don't believe him. He is getting married to Miss Hanora Clery and I'd say it's for her. It's a grand song anyway.

That's it, Cahal Hayes. I won't be able to write letters from the convent, nor receive them, so don't reply. I'm glad to be going in. The place isn't the same since you left.

With love, (if Rev. Mother saw that!).
Your friend always,
Mary Bresnan.

CHAPTER TWENTY THREE.

Wild and carefree were the three years for Garvok before his accession to leadership. He spent much of his time with Esk and the learning process was ongoing, but he was free to do much as he pleased at other times. He became very well known to everybody and was well liked also. The whispers were passed around that he would make a good leader and the tribe would regain its great power with Garvok as leader. This was not a reflection on Esk's period of rule, since that had been a 'minding-time' until Garvok's return. It was not, however, a time of expansion and conquest and the young men, in particular, wanted the excitement of cattle-raid and plunder. Careless of the consequences they looked towards exciting leadership from Garvok.

The handing over of control took place on the summer solstice three years after his return. It was a simple ceremony due to the recent death of Garaun's wife, Riac, Nefa Rua's mother and Garvok's foster-mother. She had been the steadying influence on all, from whom came direction and encouragement, and also solace and comfort when required. Garvok ached more than at Nanda's death from which he had been somewhat removed because of being in Aney. He had not been allowed to attend obsequies then. His sorrow was wild and uncontrolled, deranged and damaging until Nefa Rua came to him. Later he would realise that she came to him encouraged by Riac. As Nefa Rua had done for him, Garvok was there to help her through her spell of violent anguish. He did it with love and understanding. Holding her lovely body he wept with her and consoled her and they both realised how much they needed each other. But this only added further pain. How far from love does hatred live when barriers prevent? Only time can tell!

Garaun's sorrow was dignified. His death-wish waited in the wings until Nefa Rua's anguish would abate enough to allow her to take calm and serious control of the tribe. She was the one, the chosen one. The wisdom of choosing a successor during the lifetime of the leader was pragmatic, and was practised by the better-organised tribes, as on Aney. Even though the entitlement to leadership extended to the *derbh fine* (extended family), it very often remained with one tribal branch and descended from father to son or daughter, as in this case. Good leadership meant safety and prosperity for all the tribe and its continuance was desirable. Internal strife generally sprang from poor leadership. All knew that it was Garaun's wish that Nefa Rua should succeed him. From early age he had recognised the qualities and encouraged them. The handing over was gradual, almost contemporary with Garvok's accession. Would that Nefa Rua and Garvok could marry! Blood laws prevented but could be overturned but marriage within the *derbh fine* was known to weaken physical and mental abilities. As both became tribal leaders, marriage for them would be in the forming of an alliance with another tribe and thus ensuring support in times of difficulty. They love each other. Are they allowed to love? Does Garvok know of the love of Becan and Nanda?

The three years had passed quickly and Garvok was a mature warrior having reached his nineteenth year. His fosterage in Aney had been well spent. As well as being trained in military and hunting skills he had been educated in history and poetry, and given knowledge of family law and lineage. Esk had built on this and had instructed him on the duties of leader within the tribe and relationships with neighbouring and more distant tribes. Esk took him to visit those tribes and he was welcomed and many offers of marriage were forthcoming. Garvok's refusals caused Esk to rage. The slight to the tribe in question could deprive him of support in times of difficulty.

"You are a foolish headstrong youth," Esk would shout, "and you will pay the price."
"You are still leader, Esk, and you know that I love Nefa Rua. I want her only. We love one another."
"Love!" Esk would snap. "For you there is no love. You will lead, not love."

At such times Garvok was always alert lest the fishing-spear should loop in his direction.
"Please help us Esk!"

A plea indeed received with outward scorn but Esk would use his influence to try to make the union possible, even though the odds were greatly against it. If marrying Nefa Rua was Garvok's dream, the uniting of the tribes of Gur and Aney was a dream long entertained by Esk.

Garvok's seemingly total unconcern for his own safety was a further annoyance for Esk. The youth would go off hunting alone, dogs and spear, and not return for hours, often long past the time when worry begins. Eventually Tana asked Garvok to tell them when and where he was going and allow at least two warriors to be his guard-companions. He could not refuse her, as he knew that the request sprung from her concern for Esk. Away from the fort he could direct them as he wished.

Aney was usually his direction and thus reasonably safe. While hunting was important it was often the excuse to take

him to the holy well which was their rendezvous point, the mound above the well in actual fact.
“This is where Patrick, the holy man, slept. He blessed the water and it cures illness.”
“In Aney he would not have had to sleep under a tree,” was Nefa Rua’s provocative reply.

This was on a day in summer, a day of sunshine, of life in its fullness. His guards were resting on Knocksraher within calling distance. Garvok and Nefa Rua sat side by side on the mound happy in the warmth of their love, content in the silence, unaware that evil was afoot. It was a time of peace; attacks were so rare that it was difficult for sentries to be vigilant at all times. A dark cloud did momentarily disturb their love and happiness. Nefa Rua would later recall a shiver on her spine and a twinge of fear that was gone when the sunshine returned. The attack on Aney would change their lives forever, the attack of a renegade band. Desperate men, outcasts, they had the guile to use the most vulnerable time of the day. Afternoon! The single sentry had placed the point of his spear in the ground and was resting on the shaft, half-asleep. There is a general pause in mid-afternoon when the heat of the day swelters and the food and beer of the midday meal had over-relaxed the sentry. This is the time when hungry angry men are most alert, ready to use the advantage of time and surprise, to strike, gather and disappear.

Garaun was restless. Earlier Nefa Rua and he had allowed bitter words between them. Better to say that they disagreed strongly as to her relationship with Garvok. This had taken place as they ate together.
“I am going to meet Garvok later,” she said nonchalantly as the meal concluded.
“How I wish things could be different for you both.”

He spoke as from a distance, a dreamy apologetic tone that seemed to be far removed from the present; a weak statement from a weakening man becoming an indecisive leader.
"Why don't you allow us to be together?" The question had been asked many times.
There was no reply.
"We will be together," and anger rose within her, "and if it means that I cannot be leader of Aney, then you can choose from my brothers."
"You cannot shirk your duty. You have long known my wishes and the wishes of your tribe. Remember that it was your mother's wish also."
"No, it wasn't! She knew of our love and wanted that we be together."

He bowed his head and the single deep sigh told of his sorrow, his indecision, and Nefa Rua was angry and hurt to see the father who, to her, had embodied all the best qualities, bravery, integrity, wisdom and concern for his people, to see him so hurt by Riac's death that his judgement was flawed. She said no more but gathered her spear and left him. She knew that both were reacting to loss and she felt that she was losing twice in not being able to be with Garvok. As she crossed the hill she was overcome with regret and a great sympathy for her father came upon her. She stopped and turned but then Garvok came to mind and she knew that he would be waiting, so she went forward. This was the lost moment she would forever wish to recapture.

She told Garvok what had happened and he sensed her sadness and put his arm around her and she wept briefly.
"What will we do? We belong together. It is our destiny. We cannot deny it," she said as she stood up and walked a little

away. Garvok came behind her and held her shoulders and gently turned her about.

"We must be together and we will."

Both were sure that it would be so from that moment onwards.

The fort was never so ill prepared for an attack. The single sentry was no longer vigilant, his thoughts far removed from his task. The older folk were dozing in the sun, adding to their store for the winter days ahead. The younger women had taken the children to the river to swim and wash and cool in the heat. Some of the men were upriver patiently trying to spear fish, but within calling distance should they be needed. The bulk of the men and younger boys were off hunting. They had taken the dogs with them so that the only dogs in the fort were the old and they were sleeping in the sunshine also. Garaun was sitting out but not resting. The sun was directly in the west and he was facing it. This was just a little unusual because he normally faced east towards the eastern brow of the hill where Riac lay buried. He was worried .He wanted to talk again with Nefa Rua.

They had watched since morning from a grove on the hillside, hiding in the treetops so that the dogs would be unlikely to catch their scent. Whatever breeze there was, and indeed it was light, was from the west. The smell of cooking made them hungrier and the leader had to exercise strong control to keep them from attacking at mealtime. He had succeeded and with hunger grew aggression. They saw the women and children leaving the fort. They saw the hunters prepare and leave. They saw a beautiful young red-haired girl set out with spear in hand, saw her stop and hesitate, turn about and then decide to carry on. It took leadership again to prevent her being followed by some and lascivious whisperings filled the air. Nobody about except the sentry on his platform. The gates of the fort had been carelessly left open. They watched the sentry's stance become more and more lethargic. The time had come. They left the trees and became a disciplined attacking band. The sentry was unaware of their approach until the very last moment when instinct alerted him, only in time to be struck down by a sword blow that took his head from his shoulders. Something alerted Garaun at the same time. Turning he saw the ragged men charge into the fort. He snatched for his sword but before he could raise it a spear entered his chest, another his stomach and a sword blow split his head in two. He fell dead to the ground. His body seemed to move as the spears were roughly removed and he was stabbed again and again to the point of mutilation. The few old people who were enjoying the sunshine were similarly dealt with.

The marauders lost no men; got plenty of food and some weapons and valuables; no females, which annoyed. They were long gone when the hunters returned; when the women and children came from the river; when the wail began. They were deep in the safety of the forest when Nefa Rua returning heard the wail and felt the panic of the possibility that it was for her father.

The wail drifted on the wind before fire-signal or bone-clash. Fear is always the first reaction; it chilled all that heard and those in groups could exchange their suspicions, and few thought of Garaun. Still it was a call to involvement, to visit, to console. For a while Garvok was unconcerned. His thoughts were only with Nefa Rua, whose love he now knew.

Huge solemnity accompanied Garaun's obsequies. The mourning fire had blazed on the hilltop now for three days. A cacophony of bellowing startled the air. It came from the pen also on the hilltop where Garaun's five best cows were left unfed, a chorus of lamentation. The fire and bellowing announced burial on the third day. Garaun's killers would read the signs also and know two things. They would know that they had killed a leader and that pursuit would begin when the fires quenched. They did not know fear. Nor could they have been aware of the shocking vengeance that would be wrought on them.

It was a Christian ceremony directed by Becan's monks, but the burial was in the most southern of the hilltop barrows. There were three, just below the summit where Áine rested in her cairn, and they were already called Leaba 'n Triúr. Here Riac lay, and Ciarb and generations of leaders of the past. Nefa Rua would join them one day. The remains of the sentry and the old people who had been murdered with Garaun had been buried outside the fort on the previous day.

The internment completed, the animals were released and began to ravenously tear at the grass. Their hunger would not be sated until stomach was filled and regurgitation took place. Those who had attended the great fire were also relieved of their duties, and before sunset the fire would smoulder and quench and Garaun's spirit would be free as the wind-scattered ash. Or would it?

The leaders of the surrounding tribes had gathered. They had brought the sympathy of their people. They had come to share in the grief and to speak praises of Garaun. They saw Nefa Rua's beauty and those with eligible sons pondered and planned marriage alliance, while some cast lecherous looks and thought of her for themselves. These matters would not be discussed today, but the ground could be subtly and diplomatically prepared.

Traonach of Bruree was the most powerful leader present. While the feasting was in progress he took charge of the discussion which ranged over various tribal matters. The defence of territorial boundary was high on the list. War was a constant and even though the leaders present were generally well disposed towards one another, they tended to mind their own affairs and not get involved in disputes between others, except when the territory was threatened. So it was unusual that when Nefa Rua and Garvok joined them, that Traonach should offer help. An ulterior motive!

"Garaun's spirit cries for revenge. I will pursue his killers and deal with them, as they deserve," he said with great gravity.
The others nodded their approval, but Nefa Rua responded almost curtly,
"The time of mourning is over. The responsibility for this tribe is now mine. It brings with it the obligation to put my father's spirit to rest. While I thank you for your offer, Traonach, this duty I must do myself and I will not rest until it is done."

Her voice was firm and nobody could doubt neither her determination nor her intent. The matter was not mentioned again and in mid-afternoon the farewells and scattering took place.

The old folk offered consolation and advice and were rebuked. The young were in awe of the intensity of her anger. Warriors and workers alike were treated with derision and the feeling grew among them that she was right; that they had failed her. The elders and advisors were ignored. Nefa Rua took nobody's counsel. Garvok was barely tolerated and he saw her love for him ebb away. He grew to fear her anger. From the day of Garaun's killing she had changed from happy girlhood to dangerous hateful womanhood. Awful deeds can have awful effects.

She chose ten of her warriors. She had ordered an assembly in the fort at the spot where Garaun had died. She didn't speak, she pointed and beckoned them to come forward. It became immediately apparent that her action was cruelly motivated. True the chosen warriors were capable but they had the largest families, the biggest responsibilities. Disbelief showed on the faces of the younger warriors who should have been the chosen ones. They were responsible only to themselves in most cases and were always anxious for adventure and plunder. A ripple of whispered annoyance was quelled with a glance.

"Get your horses and weapons ready. Bring food along. We leave at dawn," was all she said.

Garvok had entered the fort and dismounted. He approached Nefa Rua.
"We leave in the morning," she said curtly.
"I will be with you…"
"No, you will not."
She left him standing there as she entered the house.

CHAPTER TWENTY FOUR.

"Cahal, you are nearly forty years of age. It is your duty to marry and raise a good Catholic family."
His friend, Fr. Tim Hannigan , also a Limerick man, and his senior by ten years, was constantly insisting and encouraging. Their friendship had developed during Cahal's deep hurt, now many years ago, when he sought solace in the taverns of Cannery Row. Though his nights were ill spent he somehow managed to drag himself to work most days. Mrs. Kenneally was terribly upset even though she was the only one who knew the extent of the hurt.
"You're destroying your health, a mhic," she would say gently as he pushed another meal aside with apologies and pretence of being unwell. Minutes later he would be in the tavern.

The day came when Mr. Talbot said,
"Master Hayes, I am disappointed with you. You came here on the recommendation of my good friend, and yours, Mr. Kenneally. You showed aptitude and ability and I quickly marked you down for promotions that would take you quickly to a top position in the business. But you have changed. You must rid yourself of whatever has done this to you. God's help is close by if only you ask."

Cahal suspected that this might be more than a reprimand and in his unsteady state he considered resigning before being dismissed. He was angry with the old man. His life was his own to do what he liked with it. He didn't expect what followed.

"In my left hand I hold a month's wages. This I am going to give you and a month's leave. But you must shake my right hand and promise me that you will return after the month freed from whatever it is that troubles you."

"I have been sacked," he thought, "but I will take the money and never come back."
Then for a brief moment he recognised the concern in the old man's eyes. It was as if he was standing before his own father. He accepted the money, hesitated and then took the proffered right hand. He knew shame and bowed his head.
"Thank you, sir, I'll do as you say."
A firm hand of encouragement gripped his shoulder.
"God be with you, boy! Come back well!"
After four or five drinks he was laughing at the foolish old man.

Mrs. Kenneally knew the reason for Cahal's sorrow. On the night of his reading the letters, he literally fell in the door and staggered into the room where she sat alone. Before she could speak he blurted out,
"She is dead! Kate is dead! Dead, dead, dead!"
Now he was on his knees by her side, telling the story between sobs. She held his hand and stroked his hair and whispered,
"Whist, lad, whist! God and Mary help you."

When he had finished he wept in a vain attempt to release his sorrow. She held his head to her breast and his tears subsided as she sang a lullaby in Irish, which he had often heard his mother sing. Peace came and he was home again and these things hadn't happened, but later as intoxic sleep came to him, the word 'Kate' was repeated over and over again. In the morning the defences were back in place and Mrs. Kenneally held the disclosures of the previous night in trust. It is said that a sorrow shared is a sorrow halved. Not so, but Cahal would be forever grateful to the older woman and he would be aware of her concern in her subtle attentions and words of encouragement.

Her husband was away on a buying trip in New York and would be away for some weeks. When Cahal hadn't returned home for five days she was at her wit's end with worry. Always very reserved she lived in her husband's shadow and rarely had to make decisions. When she could bear it no longer she went to the store and it was there she heard the story from Mr. Talbot himself. His anxiety didn't help. He advised contacting the police, and offered to, but she asked him to refrain for a couple of days.
"He will come home. I know he will," but she was not convinced.

The church was her pillar in all her needs. For years she had prayed for a child and had accepted the will of God when she did not conceive again. But Cahal had come to her and her long-stored, unused maternal instincts surfaced to her great happiness; and she was careful not to crowd him. Now she was lost again without him. She went to the church and prayed. She prayed that he would be all right, that he would come home safely, that his pain would pass.

The whispered 'Hello, Mrs. Kenneally,' startled her.
She thought for a split second that her prayer had been answered, that it was Cahal returned. The soft Irish accent belonged to Fr. Tim Hannigan, the young curate from Ireland and her very good friend.
"I'm terribly worried, Fr.," and she didn't even return his greeting.
"Is it himself? What's wrong?"
"No, Fr., it's Cahal. He hasn't come home for five days."
"Do you know where he is?"

"No, Fr. He left for work supposedly last Thursday and I haven't seen him since."
"Let's go into the presbytery and we'll have a cup of tea and a chat."

Fr. Tim and Cahal had met and were becoming friends. As he listened to the story of Kate, his priestly training rebelled but his humanity easily won. As soon as he had consoled the troubled lady and assured her that he would find Cahal, he began his search.

It took him to the strangest of places where even his priestly garb wasn't always recognisable and protecting. Young and tough enough he stepped over broken bodies, pitiful discards of the course of life. They had opted out of the regime, had escaped! But no! They had taken the wrong road and some would never get off it. Cahal was in there somewhere. Fr. Tim knew fear. He was accosted many times by the saddest of people, male and female. He was begged from, offered sex, abused, threatened and buffeted but his search was singular. He freely gave of his priesthood and dispensed charity and consolation, but it broke his heart to see so many souls ravaged, destroyed, lost. To find Cahal, however, was his objective and he did.

It was well for Cahal that Fr. Tim found him. He had escaped being press-ganged while being in a reasonably sober passage of time. He had tried to assuage his sorrow with aggression and always lost. He was battered, broken, hurt, but didn't care, wasn't conscious, just totally uncomprehending under a huge fog of sorrow, obliterating the necessity to wake in the morning and continue with living.

When he found him in the gutter Fr. Tim was treated with aggressive disdain, but the punches dissipated into tears and Cahal Hayes was rescued. He was taken to the presbytery and welcomed. He slept for two full days. He woke in a strange environment, brightness reflecting from white walls. Time passed. A beam of sunlight caught the crucifix on the wall opposite his bed and, through the dustmotes he was aware of the eyes of the crucified one. He saw accusation and it shocked him, and frightened him.

"Where am I? What am I doing here?"
He knew the answers to both.
"What can I do?"
Of that he wasn't as sure.

The first peal of the bell crashed into his consciousness and he swung his feet on to the floor, stood up, felt he weakness and fell back on the bed. He nestled into his pillows and decided to wait until Fr. Tim came. He fixed on the crucifix and saw the accusation replaced with a gentler understanding. This did not please him. His guilt would not easily go away, would never go away. Shame was with guilt and together they were controlling his life. Cahal was drifting back towards sleep. Drifting, in images of home and Mary, and then Kate, and thoughts of tender love, followed by the most abject sorrow and desolation. Tears that can flow in wake or sleep, tears pitiful, tears hopeless, and on and on to total heartbreak and on again to acceptance of sorts. The door was opened and Fr. Tim came into the room.

The priest was stern. It was now up to Cahal to choose direction. Curtains flung back and windows opened wide before,
"Up! This is it! Bathroom is there and clean clothes. When you've bathed and dressed you can either stay here and work

for a few weeks, or, and it's your choice, walk out and go back to where I found you. I will not follow."
Neither greeting nor farewell but the slammed door spoke and Cahal understood.

Cahal Hayes recovered. Emotionally seriously wounded to the point of scars permanent, he worked the rungs of the ladder to the 'top' and became a wealthy man and still remained alone and hurt and lonely.

CHAPTER TWENTY FIVE.

Fury! Fury triggering abject and awful change! Thus did Nefa Rua carry the burden of guilt into a total transformation of personality. Even though she had rejected Garvok and his offer of help, he was at her fort at daybreak with five of his best warriors. She chose to ignore them and they followed at a short distance. Some two hours after departure they reached a cluster of unprotected houses, on the margin of very poor land. These people were barely able to eke out a living, were weak and harmless and of the lowest social order. On these helpless people she chose to vent her anger. The savagery of her unprovoked attack led Garvok through disbelief to despair, to non-recognition of the wonderful girl of his love.

These simple people could not have expected and were totally unprepared for the brutality visited on them. They knew Nefa Rua by sight and reputation, they knew of Garuan's death. They would have expressed sympathy and helped if they could, but they did not get a chance.
"Who killed Garaun?" abrupt, sharp, intimidatory.
"Did they come by here?"
"Did you shelter them?"

The poor confounded attempts to answer went unheard as blood lust exploded from Nefa Rua's hand in cleaving the old leader's head from his body. Garvok and his men stood in stunned non-comprehension of such actions. His orders had been very explicit as to when force could and should be used. Not in these circumstances! Even Nefa Rua's warriors were briefly stunned, but her action allowed this irrational onslaught on innocent people and values were set aside as the warriors wrought havoc and death. By the time she called halt there were ten people dead and the others had run screaming into the bog. She had stopped short of allowing her men to rape the young women. There would be no revenge for the murdered. Their step on the social ladder did not carry an honour price. With heavy heart Garvok led his men away under a barrage of insult.

The great lake lies between two great hills, which bring the great river back to river-shape. Above it the lake stretches up and up to the north, to great length and sometimes to great width. The many islands can be homes for people or refuges for outcasts. The killers of Garaun had one such island-refuge. Knowing that Nefa Rua was in pursuit and aware of her intent, they deemed that the island on the great lake would shelter, and allow the danger to pass. Wild disgraced outcasts, consciousless killers constantly pursued, their instinct of self-preservation was alert at all times. On hearing of Nefa Rua's savage attack they were frightened enough to seek shelter. How the actions of one or more can influence and change a personality, a life, and its extension into tribe and community, can only be viewed through the retrospect of history. If the deed had been recorded then it would merely say that Garaun of Aney was slain by a renegade band. That is not a good account of a death and a more enlightened chronicler would glorify the moment. He would record a struggle and a brave resistance and the killing of some before being overcome. Thus was Garaun's death reported. The record would be soon forgotten in the actions of his daughter on her trail of revenge.

The news of her first violence spread ahead and she was allowed to cross territories without interference. In some cases this resulted from fear but, for many families who had suffered at the hands of the renegade band, Nefa Rua was seen as the one to avenge and punish. In the foothills of the mountains to the northeast she conferred with the chieftain of Maigh Rua. He was a kinsman through marriage and he and Garaun had been good friends for many years. He had not attended the burial, being in conflict with a neighbouring tribe at the time. The matter had been resolved and he had intended visiting Aney but Nefa Rua' s coming removed the need. He was quite disturbed as he expressed his sympathy and loss. He was also impressed by the courage of the young girl forced into leadership by cowardly action, and her undeviating intent on revenge. The harsh personality did not fit one so beautiful and young. Talk of Garaun mollified her just a little but she quickly reverted to her singular purpose.

"I did not come here for advice," in a tone charged with emotion. "All I want is knowledge of where his killers might be."
"Like it or not you will be given advice by me. I owe it to your father. Do you not realise that at times that band could be thirty forty strong. What chance would you have against them?"
She did not answer, but asked,
"Where do they shelter when they are being pursued?"
"Mostly on an island on Lough Derg, close to the northern shore, most of three days ride from here."
"Can you give me a guide to lead us there?"
"Yes, but I still think that you are unwise."
"We will rest outside your fort and set out at dawn."

He knew that it was pointless to invite her in, her mind was made up. Before going to sleep when the quiet of the night brought her a moment of stillness and peace, she reflected on the chieftain's words and chided herself for her impetuosity. Garvok also came to mind. Thoughts of love came, were quickly dismissed but not before a tear being shed.

The rage had returned by morning and they set out, using the lesser-used ways. They headed for the mountains to the east of the lake. The idea was to avoid other tribes and even single or clustered homesteads as much as possible. At the approach of horses the rural dwellers fled for shelter, fearing that they were to be subjected to attack, being the main victims of renegade bands. Just before nightfall on the second day they crested a hill and looked down on the lake. The guide pointed to an island with plenty of tree-cover, roughly two hundred paces from the shore.

"That it is," and the guide turned his horse for home.
"Wait!"she called as she held out a piece of gold to him.
"Be very careful!" he warned in gratitude. 'There is no smoke, no sign of life, but it is often only in the dark of night that a fire is lighted, and in a place where the flames cannot be seen. They may well be in there waiting if they are aware of your coming. The best thing to do is to find a boat or use a strong swimmer to cross over in the darkness. If you wish I will do it for you, but in the meantime we must remain out of sight."

Her first reaction was to refuse his help and dismiss him, but she also knew that her men had little or no experience of water other than a swim in the river.
"Are you familiar with water?" she asked.
"Though I now live in Maigh Rua I spent the first eighteen years of my life on this lakeshore. That is why I was chosen to guide you."
"Then I will accept your help and reward you for it."

Halra was the guide's name. True to his word he waited until dark and swam to the island. Impatiently Nefa Rua awaited his return.

"They are there," he reported as dawn began to break behind them. "I was very close to the camp and the fire was lighting. There seemed to be plenty of food but a great unease and disagreement was there also. It seemed that the authority of their leader was being questioned. It sprang from Garaun's killing. The killing of the sentry was not even mentioned, but to kill the leader of a tribe meant pursuit and revenge. They had only realised what they had done when they observed the burial from a distant hill."

"How many of them are there?" she interrupted.

"As many as thirty young and old, and three or four women."

"We will attack them on the island."

"That would not be wise."

"It isn't wisdom I seek but revenge in blood," as battle fury flashed in her eyes.

"Then it is time that I left. I have done as I promised," and his eyes flashed also. He was not subject to her authority. He turned to walk away, then stopped.

"You must catch them unawares if you are to have any chance against them. They outnumber you well. From what I overheard they will not remain on the island much longer. They will cross to the mainland within the next couple of days. They will do this before sunrise. They will swim across leading their horses behind them. Attack them as they come ashore and the advantage will be yours."

He mounted his horse and rode away.

Nefa Rua knew that she had received good advice. She regretted Halra's departure and knew that it was her own impatience and intransigence that had driven him away.

"Anyway it isn't his fight," she reminded herself.

It was now time to plan, to form an attack strategy. The anger was put aside and her qualities of leadership surfaced.

She chose the best position from which to observe the island unseen; hers would be the watch before dawn. She briefed her warriors. No longer aloof and insulting, she was once again their friend and little by little their enthusiasm for battle and revenge equalled her own.

Halra was right. They began to leave the island on the third morning when the fingers of dawn touched the sky. She quickly alerted her warriors. From the coppice in which they remained undercover, they could all observe a wait for the order to attack. Fifteen men gathered on the island shore. Each led a horse on a long rein. Weapons, perhaps spoils, and probably food were tied on the horses' backs. Five men entered the water, pulling hard on the reins while those on shore slapped the horses' haunches. Soon the men were swimming, horses following. As the first five reached shore, the second group of five entered the water. On shore the reins were tidied, weapons removed, as the horses shook themselves to remove the water. The second five reached shore. The third were halfway across when Nefa Rua launched the attack.

With bloodcurdling shouts and screams they swept down on the unprepared renegades and a cast of spears impaled six bodies, and death hastened by savage sword blows. Spears were withdrawn as the four recovered from the initial shock and had grouped together and fought from the ground and cast their spears. Two pierced the advancing horses, which led to wild whinnying and disarray, the other two found their mark. One entered a warrior's throat, which would certainly result in his death. He fell from his horse and lay on the ground, hands wildly trying to extricate himself. The struggle didn't last long and, if one had time to observe, the fact that he made no sound was eerily strange. The second warrior was wounded in the thigh and he was able to withdraw the spear and cast it back and it took its toll. The noise of unequal battle is different. The few remaining renegades were shouting at their five companions in the water to come ashore to their aid. They had changed direction when the attack came; not back to the island where they knew their presence was now known, but further down the shore from where they could mount and attack, or escape which was more to the point in the circumstances as they saw it. Nefa Rua saw what was happening and sent three of her men to head them off. There was no real resistance anymore. The shout 'Garaun' was heard again and again. The leader had remained in the shelter of his men but now they were mostly dead or dying. He stood alone with spear and sword with fear and battle fury mixed. She signalled that it would be her duty and privilege to kill him herself. She leaped from her horse, threw her spear down and moved towards him, sword held high. He cast his spear, which she easily evaded. Their swords clashed again and again. He retreated but she had underestimated his strength and agility. A fierce upstroke caught her unawares, and the tip of the blade pierced jaw and cheek, blinded her right eye and gashed open her forehead, She fell to the ground. Her men killed the renegade leader. Revenge had been gained but at a price!

CHAPTER TWENTY SIX

True for Fr. Tim! Cahal was nearly forty, was forty and the years continued one, two and three and he had not married. Nor did he move house when he could well have afforded to. The old Young Irelander, John Kenneally died. Cahal remained with Mrs. Kenneally and perhaps it was in her mothering that his solace lay. She did hint that he should marry but really meant that it should be after her death. She died and left him in sorrow. As had been Mr Kenneally's will and testament, Cahal inherited the house and a fairly substantial sum of money. He raised a monument over their graves, sent some more money home to Séamus and was generous to the Church. He also gave to members of the Salvation Army who were working with the homeless and down-and-outs. He knew what it was like and would continue to help all through his life. By now Cahal Hayes was a wealthy man. When he had returned to work all those years ago, he did so with a compulsion and an intensity that drove him harder and harder. Work was his life, his refuge, and his efforts were appreciated and promotion followed promotion. The ageing Mr. Talbot depended more and more on Cahal. By the age of forty he was general manager with few steps left.

The year was now 1896. After Mrs. Kenneally's death his own parents became more of a concern. It was now twenty-four years since he had left home. The call was strong. To see his aged parents, Séamus, his sisters, to stand on the lakeshore, to climb the hills. More and more, each day the call became stronger. It was time.
"Mr. Talbot," he began one morning, "I want to go home to Ireland to see my parents before they too die."

Cahal would never be sure whether it was a smile or a frown crossed the old man's face, but he heard the reply with gladness.
"Yes, Mr. Hayes, that you must do. I will conduct the business while you are away, but on condition that you will return and take complete charge, from the presidential chair."
"He never fails to surprise me," was Cahal's happy thought.

Neither his father nor Séamus was at the station of Knocklong to meet him. That was how he wanted it, so that he could see Lough Gur briefly alone and measure life against the passage of the twenty plus years. The jarvey mixed his pretended subservience of bowing and cap touching with a healthy curiosity about American life and of Cahal's position there. The trappings, he saw, were in keeping with the demeanour of 'the fine gentleman.'

"Lough Gur. Of course I'll take you there. Wouldn't a drink out of the lake do old Moll the best of good."
"So you can take me there?"
"O Cinnte! Cinnte! Cinnte! And…let me guess! Would you be one of the Moores? …or the Hannans?"
Each time Cahal shook his head.
"One of the Fitzgeralds then? We hear that one of them is moving into politics in Boston. Are you him?"
"No! I'm not. I'm Cahal Hayes from Lough Gur and I live in San Francisco and it is over twenty years since I left home. This is my first trip home."
"Shake my hand, sir!" the jarvey beamed. "Aren't we cousins, only three times removed through my Aunt Kit and the Sheehans, cousins of your father's people. Cinnte! It's grand to be welcoming home a successful member of the family."

They were on their way. The pace was slow and between bouts of intensive conversation there was time to remember. The stone balls were still on the piers of Kilfrush and soon Hospital was reached.

"The fair is on tomorrow," Dan Dooley the jarvey, remarked, observing the barricading of shop and house fronts " to protect against the collisions and secretions of cattle in the morning, and collisions and drunken fighting of their owners in the evening" and Dan laughed heartily while throwing jibes at the erectors from his high-perched seat. No need to stop at Knockainey and Lough Gur was reached amid Dan's torrent of talk. The church, the school, the neighbours' houses, but there were only youngsters on the road. They didn't know him but he heard 'The Yank' from their lips. That Cahal was coming home was well known. They would carry the news quickly home. The children on the road nearest his home were Séamus' and when they saw the jarvey they ran as fast as their bare feet would carry them shouting,
"He's here! He's here! not Tá sé ag teacht! Tá sé ag teacht!"
"Even down here the aul' language is gone," and there was a sadness in Dan's voice.

There are moments so personal that they belong in the deepest prison of heart and mind. As Cahal walked down the passage to his home the years slipped away and a dream came true when he saw his 'old' father and mother at the door. They were dressed in their best clothes to welcome their son home. The moment transcended reality, was sacred, and was holy. The spark kindled and they became young, or at least Cahal didn't see them as old. As his mother held him he heard the whispered,
"Cahal! Cahal! Buíochas le Dia" and he held her until the weeping turned to sighs. Behind her back he held his

father's strong hard-worked hand in his office-soft one and the joy of being with his parents brought thoughts of 'why did I ever go away?', followed by flashes of the shield and Old James and young Séamus. The answer came when Séamus' admiring gaze locked eyes with his. He stood behind his father with his wife at his side and the two girls and the boy peeping from the shelter of her skirts. She would soon give birth to their fourth child. The money sent from America allowed Séamus to marry for 'love' and happiness and contentment radiated from them both.

Dan had unloaded the trunk and stood waiting. More used to the sadness of farewells he was pleased to observe the happiness of successful return. When the opportunity arose he came closer.

"When are you…?" he stammered, "or are you going back?"

"A short visit," Cahal replied, "just two weeks" as he handed Dan a more than generous payment.

"Go raibh míle …thank you very much, sir," and then impulsively, "do you want me to call for you on that day?"

"No thanks, Dan. I'm sure my brother will take me there."

"It must be a great country," Dan mused as he warmly shook Cahal's hand.

Nora, Séamus' wife, spoke, as he was about to leave.

"Come in! The tay is made. Come in Cahal and you too, Mr. Dooley. You have a long road before you back to Knocklong."

The kitchen was bright and sparkling clean. The general furnishings were as he had remembered them but the hand of the younger woman was there in the sparkling crockery and fine willow-pattern dishes, inherited from her grandmother. The large brass oil-lamp hung suspended from the ceiling ready to brighten the night. The Sacred Heart picture still had its little lamp with the red globe before it and the statue of the Blessed Virgin was on the shelf in the corner. The servant-girl was busy at the big pot over the fire preparing gruel for the younger farm animals. The biggest change for Cahal was the permanent occupation of his old parents at each side of the hob. Séamus had written as to how their days were spent and as they settled into their respective corners Cahal thanked God that he was home to see them, to find them alive and fairly well. The parlour door was open in half-apology, but the tea was served in the kitchen in deference to the old people. They passed through the parlour each night and morning going to and from their bedroom. Grown so used they scarcely looked at the wall decorations, almost unchanged since Cahal's departure. There were a few photographs or daguerreotypes of the last generation, but the dominance belonged to Daniel O'Connell, the Liberator, and Robert Emmett the darling of Ireland, and the Manchester Martyrs amid a scatter of shamrocks and harps. During his time at home Cahal would see and look and see again and wonder if the dreams of these men could be realised. There was one new picture, which Cahal hadn't previously seen and that was of Charles Stewart Parnell. It had been on the wall but was there no longer and was a source of anger and disagreement between the old man and woman. The removal from the wall and allowing it to remain in the corner was a difficult compromise to which the parish priest was a party. But the aggravation remained because, at every opportunity the old man turned it face out, only to be turned back in again by the old woman mumbling, "that disgraceful man!"

The tea, the home-made soda bread, the being home and yet he knew the feeling of being a stranger among his own.
"Tomorrow will be different. Tomorrow I'll be Cahal Hayes of Lough Gur again."
Can it be?

The boys of his youth, his friends, have either emigrated, as he had done, or are farming and raising families and caring for parents, as was Séamus. Their attitude to Cahal would be bereft of the warmth and acceptance that he has hoped to return to. That he was the finder of the Sun Shield was acknowledged. He would be forever its finder, the story of the finding be told and retold and his name remembered and the findspot pointed to. He was back home now, a rich man! The Shield was lucky! It was, wasn't it?
Of course it was! It was…it was….it was……

Sleep wasn't easy to find. In a way he regretted that he could not have returned to what was, to being in his own room with Séamus. But Séamus had Nora now in his room, and the cries were gentle, children tossing in sleep as thoughts and images implode. Barely cladding himself as the first light brightened the little window, he moved to the kitchen. Kneeling by the hearth his father was encouraging the ash-covered embers to flame. Then the kettle would boil and the first tea of the day be made. The first cup would be for the old woman, delivered to the bedroom and greeted mostly with waking groan and complaint and silence. The sleeping dog awoke, stretched and once-wagged his tail as the old man's opened the door to leave him out in the yard. As he turned back he saw Cahal.

"Móra dhuit ar maidin, a mhic," but Cahal couldn't recall the response and replied with "Good morning, father," and he was annoyed with himself. There were lots of other benedictions to be exchanged as Nora, Séamus and then the children shyly entered. Neither was Cahal comfortable among them as yet, so he answered the call of lake and hill.
"I'll walk before breakfast," he said quietly, taking his hat and coat from the rack by the door, also his cane.

He crossed O'Brien's field to reach the causeway at Black Castle. It was milking time and he did not want to interrupt the work. He would visit the O'Briens later. On to the hill and into the realms of remembrance, happy remembrance. Images of home and growing-up, of parents and family, of friends, of Mary, of Sun Shield and Séamus, of old James, and in came Kate, intruding but sadly welcome

"She should be by my side," and sadness filled his thoughts. Threatened misery is dispelled by beauty of place and shortness of breath on the rise of the hill. He doffs coat, fingers collar, expands chest and pushes for the top. On Carraig an Iolair he stands tall, tosses hat and cane in the air, shouts a mighty shout and is home again.

With new verve in step he sure-foots down the hill, striding past Ash Point and Bolin Island. Bourchier's Castle is stately among the trees. Another pull up to Carraig Aille. A strident shout from the fort startles him.

"Cahal Hayes! Cahal! Up here! Come up here!"

He recognises the 'Poet'. Owen Bresnan is calling him. The gate is too high to vault though he feels like trying. They embrace. They laugh. They slap shoulders.

"You did you bit for the 'cause', Cahal Hayes, that letter was important and freedom is ever closer."

Cahal wonders what the Poet is doing on Carraig Aille so early in the morning but doesn't ask. Perhaps that's what poets do, where poets go. The two men sit on the west wall, looking down on what was the Small Lake. They light their pipes.

"Twas down there you found it," Owen says.

"Down there," Cahal replies, pointing but he didn't really want to talk about it. The Poet did.

"They were living up here. Why did they give the Sun Shield to the lake?"

Cahal didn't answer. The clear day and sunshine would make for a day, as was the day on which he had found the shield. There are things one cannot forget. A pause, matches struck, smoke rising.
"Fitzgerald's house is quiet now." Owen was looking towards the thatched cottage on the verge of the bog. "You met some of the family in Boston?"
"I visited with them for a while and would have remained in Boston were it not for that letter."
"That's what I meant when I said you did your share for the 'cause.' It was safer to move you west."
"Johnny is doing well in politics. He was studying medicine in Harvard until his father, Cocky Tom, died and he had to become the provider for the family. I will visit him on my way back to San Francisco."
"Give them all our best regards and tell them that there will always be a welcome here at home," and the mood changed again.
" Marconi! He has sent messages to America without using the cable form Valentia Island. Isn't it amazing! The world is getting smaller by the day."
Cahal rose.
"I had better be going, Owen."
"You want to ask me about Mary, but you will not. Nor will you have to because I'll tell you. She is well and happy but I miss her. There is nobody to sing 'The Coolin' now. 'The Maid of sweet Lough Gur' is gone and 'Teampall Nua' is still. She always asks about you, Cahal." And then, "Why have you not married, Cahal?" a question that would remain unanswered.

The hand was offered and accepted and Cahal headed down the steep western slope towards home and breakfast.
"I'll give your regards to Mary."
He raised his arm but didn't turn around.

His father and Séamus agreed on the Parnell issue and that was good. The condemnation of the Catholic Church had divided the people. Cahal was proud of his father. Most men of his age would have succumbed to the direction of their priests, but since the O'Grady Agitation and the involvement and imprisoning of Fr. Matt Ryan, and the evictions, the people of Lough Gur were strongly pro-Parnell. They were devastated at his death.
"Ah, Cahal, 'twas a sad day when he died. His heart was broken when they turned his people against him," and his father's slow speech was filled with sadness.
"He won the land for us, himself and Mr. Davitt," Séamus added. "The Count's estate will be part of the next Land Act and then we will own our land at last."
"Count de Salis is a good landlord," the old man said, "but it is right that we should own our land, isn't it, Cahal?"
Cahal nodded in agreement, and in happiness that the land question was being favourably resolved.

During Cahal's stay the three had many discussions and were often joined by the neighbours. To some Cahal was a friend of youth, to others he would always be the finder of the Sun Shield, the lucky one! He had succeeded in the New World and was in possession of a great fortune, it was said. They drank his whiskey and questioned and dreamed. The Poet was invariably there and his radical ideas often annoyed the older men and led to heated argument, often to the point of blows threatened if not struck. They spoke of Home Rule, he of full freedom and independence. The priest came but didn't join in these discussions. He obeyed his superiors.

Cahal worried about his mother. Old age was taking its toll but it was more than that. She was the one who had to hand over control of her home to Séamus' wife, Nora. It was not easy, not after nearly forty years. She had done it with a restrained dignity, reluctant yet knowing what was right. She approved of Nora and was happy for Séamus, but a battle of wills had to be. It was gentle, yet meaningful, partially ignited on occasion, but Nora was firm and prevailed. The older woman retreated to the corner beside the fire, the side where the bellows was. From there she controlled the fire, a tactical position in any house. It wasn't the same for his father. Strength and good health allowed him to stand with Séamus in the working of the farm. If he had difficulty with some of Séamus' new approaches he did not say so. It was a good time, an exciting time. Soon Séamus would own the land, which had supported generations of Hayes'. It was a good time for a young man to be working the land, to be improving the land without fear of rent increase. And it was good for Séamus to have his father by his side.

"She's not as well as she should be," his father said as if reading Cahal's thoughts as they walked among the new crop of calves. The years had brought change. The place remained the same

"She was lonely after you, Cahal," he continued, "and she was afraid for you because of the Sun Shield"'

"I have sat with her and she pokes the fire and calls to the maid to put on more turf, or wet the tea, and she turns the bellows and I know that she doesn't know me anymore."

"A mhic, her concern is for you. She worries that you are alone in that far-off land. 'Why isn't he married? Why hasn't he a wife top care for him? Children of his own? Why?' That's all she says."

A pang struck his heart when he heard 'children of his own.' Nobody knew. Did they?

Cahal thought of pursuing, of probing, of Kate dead and young Kate living and 'of his own' and.... But he knew that

that part of his life was not known. It was at that moment that he resolved that he would find young Kate Hennessy on his return to America. He would find *his* daughter. Now he longed for the day of his return.

“She’s not in good health,’ his father was still talking about his mother. ‘Her rosary and the ‘díonacht’* and sometimes she sees Séamus’ children and thinks they are her own, but mostly she minds the fire.”

Cahal felt and understood his father’s sadness but the conversation had resolved an indecision that had haunted him for many years.

*Water from St. Patrick’s Well, rich in curative properties, and depended on by the old people to heal all ills.

CHAPTER TWENTY SEVEN.

Garvok was unaware of Nefa Rua's injuries. Almost everyday he either went himself to Aney or sent a messenger, but there was no news for over two weeks. Then the eight surviving warriors returned. The loss of their two companions left two families in deep mourning. When they reported on Nefa Rua there was further sadness and none could say for sure that she would recover. Her wounds had become infected and had not a wise woman tended her she would most likely have died also. On the woman's advice they took her to a convent adjoining the great monastery on the Shannon. This was in the centre of Ireland, they were told, and Saint Kieran had founded the monastery many centuries previously. It was fortunate that Halra had had a change of mind and had come back to lead them back to Maigh Rua. Some kinsmen gave him a boat and they travelled north on the river. Nefa Rua's warriors soon became oarsmen under Halra's instruction.

The nuns took her into their care and she quickly responded to their ministering. The infection was halted and the physical cure process began, but the disfigurement was permanent and she would bear it as a badge of her failure. Bad though it was, the mental scarring was worse. She had failed to kill the leader and the fact that it was done by one of her warriors pained. That she would have died were it not for that warrior's action was irrelevant. Moments since and in many moments to come, in the silence of her inner turmoil, she would wish that she had died rather than to have to bear the double burden of failure and disfigurement. It would lead to a permanent change in personality. Her anger, which followed Garaun's killing, should have been dissipated by the deaths of the renegades, but no! It would not be so.

It was almost so but circumstances contrived to prevent her rehabilitation, but not just yet. The nun who cared for her was a gentle creature of her own age. She gave Nefa Rua her friendship and her love and ignored the many times these gifts were rejected. Her name was Clara and she had chosen a life in religion, having had great difficulty in persuading her father to allow her. He too was a chieftain and her arranged marriage would form an alliance with another tribe. She managed to convince him and to get his blessing in the end. In the early days when the fever raged, she sat by the bedside and comforted Nefa Rua, holding her when her body convulsed with pain and anguish and her cries were for the dead Garaun and the lost Garvok. And friendship developed and grew stronger and after a time the disfigurement was no longer a subject not for mention.

"You were blessed with the three great beauties, of body and mind and spirit," Clara would say. "One is slightly damaged, only slightly, but the others remain intact. They will be your strength and God will bless you."

She taught her to pray the Christian prayer and Nefa Rua rediscovered the gentler side of life as they gathered flowers on the riverbank and watched the industry of water birds. They exchanged stories of their early lives and they were not without similarities, and there was laughter. They giggled at the overtures of shy admirers and spoke of love because Clara had also loved but it was a love that could not be. Of course these things did not happen until she had recovered physically. With Clara she had again found the calm lost on the day of Garaun's killing. The abbess observed the change and allowed Clara to spend as much time as she wished with Nefa Rua.

Nefa Rua's concern for affairs at Aney declined as she found peace with Clara among the community of nuns. She had sent instructions with her warriors that her brother, Ciarbach, should be chieftain until her return. Weeks to months and the messengers brought news of affairs in Aney where all was well. They also brought messages from Garvok. As yet she was unable to respond to these, other than to send verbal greetings to all including Garvok. The messengers brought back news also of her well-being and of great change (the disfigurement was never mentioned). Speculation grew that Nefa Rua would remain in the convent, and she began to think on those lines herself also. Meanwhile Garvok languished as he realised that Nefa Rua had become again the girl he had known and loved. Should he visit her? After much soul-searching he decided that he would wait her return.

A year passed! Whereas Nefa Rua had not voiced an intention to join the community of nuns, she partook in all activities as if she was one of them. She prayed at all the prayer gatherings of the day in the chapel, was given daily duties with the others and performed them with happiness and enthusiasm. Generally she was paired with Clara, but not always. The abbess tested her and found that her acceptance of the most menial tasks showed generous spirit. Now Clara prayed that Nefa Rua would stay.

"I may as well stay," Nefa Rua would say, "no man would have me now, not a disfigured hag like me," as she fingered the mark left by the awful wound, and sometimes thought of Garvok.

"You have not lost your beauty," Clara would counter. "God has blessed you in many ways."
"I'm ugly, ugly!" and sometimes a tear.

This led one day to Clara telling her the story of St. Bridget, who had asked God to make one side of her face ugly so that she could present it to her suitors and thus avoid their attentions. Nefa Rua was pleased and resolved to accept what could not now be changed .She did think for a time that if God could make Bridget ugly he could also remove her mark, but she knew it would not happen.

"Let us make a veil to cover this mark," Clara suggested one day as she was combing Nefa Rua's long red hair. She drew the hair across the face to hide the disfigurement.
"It can be done so easily and your beauty will be restored"' Clara continued as Nefa Rua looked at her reflection in the clear water. This was the first time she could do so without anguish and revulsion.
"Can we?" was her simple question.

Clara had this long planned and was ready to get to work. She had also decided that the veil would be white, almost as if it was for a young girl entering the convent. But as well as covering the head it also had to cover half the face. In fact it was not nun-like at all when it was finished because Clara made sure that the red hair was visible even on the forehead and the veil hid the damaged part of the face. The transformation was achieved and beauty reborn.

Miles away on Carraig Aille Garvok was greatly saddened when Tana died and Esk soon followed. He had been ten years older than Tana and so had lived a long life. Without his counsel Garvok was now ruling alone. He did it well and only his loneliness at the absence of Nefa Rua brought some unhappiness. Perhaps she would never return. When one year passed into two Esk told him that he should seek a woman elsewhere. He did. She was an older woman, a widow from a strong tribe living to the north of Gur. She did not become pregnant even though she had borne previously and after a year she returned to her people. She could do this without shame, the implication being that Garvok was at fault. Their marriage portions were divided. Garvok took a young slave-girl into his house. She took care of his needs and bore a child. They awaited the return of Nefa Rua. It was a time of prosperity and relative calm. On Aney the situation was similar.

Likewise at Clonmacnoise where the pace of life was much faster. Not so in the shelter of the convent, but on the perimeter of the monastery where the great river Shannon was crossed by a great wooden bridge. Over this bridge a constant stream of traffic crossed east and west. And dealings were ever afoot with animals (and indeed slaves) exchanged, produce and implements bartered and bought, a hub of activity. There, also, passed entertainers and mendicant friars, not always welcomed by the monastery monks. Great was the excitement when a king and his entourage crossed, usually escorted by spear-wielding warriors on horseback or on foot with banners aflutter and trumpets announcing arrivals and departures. The crafty monks knew how to collect their tolls which, when added to the generous endowments for passage to heaven and shriving of sin, filled the monastery coffers. Nefa Rua remained mesmerised by it all, and at peace. She was free of the restrictions of the convent and often mingled among the people at the crossing. The veil gave her a mysterious air and led to conjecture. Rumours abounded and on one occasion a young prince pursued her to the convent gates and would only leave when Clara lied that she would be Sister Nefa very soon.

"And you said that no man would look at you," Clara scoffed teasingly.
"It would be very easy to change matters. I almost removed the veil. That would have quickly changed his mind."
They laughed but it was somewhat forced as other thoughts entered their heads.
From Clara, "Maybe the time has come for you to become a nun with us. The direction of your life would be clear and positive."
From Nefa Rua, and not without some anger, "When I need to take that decision I will. Now is not the time."
"You know you can stay here as long as you please. You are happy among us and are greatly loved by all the sisters and we are happy for you. But I know that duty still calls to you. Aney awaits and I know that Garvok is never too far from your thoughts."
Quietly, "I don't know! My dreams died, were dashed in violence and I cannot rebuild them. I'm afraid to lose again. This time it would be the peace I have found here. Can I chance losing that too?"

The setting sun turned the river to gold. The bell was being rung from the top of the round tower. The churches and cells were bathed in the rays of sunset. For once nobody was crossing the bridge. The cattle and sheep grazed contentedly on the water meadows. The chanting of the monks reached their ears.
"It is time for us to pray also," Clara spoke in a whisper lest voice should shatter the moment.
"Pray and you will decide for the best."
Nefa nodded and followed.

The community of nuns, and Nefa Rua, huddled in the chapel and prayed for deliverance. The monastery was under attack, under brutal pagan attack. It had come in the late afternoon and without warning. Three longboats came ashore by the bridge. Nothing unusual about that! The longboats of the Fingals were a frequent sight on the river. They contributed to trade at the river crossing, but today it was different. They had come to plunder and had come at the quietest time, the time of evening prayer. Even the gates leading to the monastic settlement were not as yet closed for the night. Thirty forty heavily armed ruthless men met no resistance as they maimed and killed whomsoever they encountered. The students, who fled from their cells, were cut down within the compound. Some few managed to escape over the stockade and sought refuge in the countryside or in the high river reeds. These were peace-loving young people, many from distant lands, no match for bloodthirsty plunderers. The monks perished in the churches. The church ware was collected and all valuables, including bridge crossing tariffs. Buildings were set on fire, fuelled with priceless manuscripts. No one had had time to gain the safety of the round tower, so unprecedented was the attack.

They had come fortified with alcohol and continued to consume throughout the slaughter. Now they were wild animals unleashed, sated in blood, all-conquering. Convents and veils did not protect womanhood from them. There was resistance only from Nefa Rua, as the younger nuns were selected and the older ones murdered. The roars and shouts of the attackers were in sharp contrast to the quiet prayers of intercession of the nuns. Nefa Rua, unarmed, still fought furiously, veil dislodged she was beaten into semi-consciousness, stripped and raped again and again. The other young nuns were treated likewise.

Some weeks later, half-starved and barely clad, dirty and torn and haggard Nefa Rua staggered into Aney. The sentry, who accosted her, nearly struck her with his sword. Some instinct prevented, some splink of recognition. Nefa Rua had come home. She didn't leave her house for the best part of a full year.

CHAPTER TWENTY EIGHT.

Cahal disembarked in New York and set out for Boston on the following day. He had wired of his impending visit to Johnny, and he was on the platform to meet him. They greeted each other boisterously. But Johnny had not come alone.

" She was Mary Josephine Hannan but she is now Mrs. John Francis Fitzgerald. I introduce you to my good friend, Cahal Hayes from Lough Gur, Ireland."
"That's where Daddy is from," in high excitement as she offered her hand.
"He will be pleased to meet Cahal, and we will call on him this evening," Johnny said and then added,
"This is the only girl, Cahal, that I ever wanted to marry and now we have three children Rose, Mary Agnes and Thomas and we want you to be godfather to our next born, which will be next year. We want you to be there. A man from Lough Gur with us will mean good luck!"
Cahal nodded and they hugged and slapped backs again and Mary Josephine 'tut-tutted' at their childish behaviour.

Johnny and Cahal had much to tell each other. Both were young successful men. Johnny told Cahal all about life in politics. With the help of Matthew Keany, the neighbourhood boss in Boston's North End, he eloquently entered the arena. Johnny Fitz (James Francis Fitzgerald) became 'Honey Fitz' as with fine tenor voice he concluded his hustings with '*Sweet Adeline*' and '*When Johnny comes marching home again.*' They walked again through Boston Common, this time without being called "muckers" and they laughed as they recalled that particular incident. They were not the happy youths of twenty plus years ago; they were

mature men, serious about the world but light-hearted together.
"It will take me a few more years, Cahal, but one day I will be Mayor of Boston."
And Cahal knew that he would.

He was more convinced when he attended the meeting when Matthew Keany began his re-election campaign. It fell to Johnny to introduce (as if introduction was needed) Keany on that night. A big gathering, a band playing, flag waving and the general razzmatazz of election fever. He extolled the virtues and abilities of his boss to such an extent that anybody listening could hardly justify a vote for anyone else. But the hecklers were there as ever and Johnny effortlessly fielded all the remarks and questions. One big Irishman shouted,
"Where are your people from, Fitz?"
"All the way from poor old Ireland, like yourself, my friend. And where are you from?"
"County Mayo," was spat out.
Johnny bowed his head, blessed himself and said,
"The same county as my poor old mother, may the Lord have mercy on her soul," and a silence settled on the crowd.
Mayo! Cahal was aghast. That was until Johnny winked discreetly and the roguery was clear.
"He has it! He surely has!" and Cahal winked back.
More heckling followed but now the shouts rose, "'Sweet Adeline! Give us 'Sweet Adeline', Honey!"
He did and they joined in and he had them 'eating out of his hand.' The way was clear for Keany.

'Honey Fitz' but he would always be Johnny as far as Cahal was concerned. Their conversations were long and centred much on Ireland and the political scene. He bombarded Cahal with questions about Parnell and Davitt and the Land

League. He was particularly interested in the Plan of Campaign, the Herbertstown Agitation and the treatment of Captain Boycott. Cahal was able to quote from Parnell's speech in Ennis in 1880 when he told the people how the 'land-grabbers' should be treated:

'When a man takes a farm from which another has been evicted you must shun him on the roadside when you meet him – you must shun him in the streets of the town – you must shun him in the shop – you must shun him in the fairgreen and in the market place, and even in the place of worship, by leaving him alone, by putting him into a moral Coventry, by isolating from the rest of his country as if he were the leper of old – you must show him your detestation of the crime he has committed.'

"Powerful! Powerful! Say it again, Cahal," as he urgently wrote down the words.

"He is called the Uncrowned King of Ireland. He has served his country well."

"But he is happy with Home Rule" Johnny countered.

"There is a good result to the Land League. The tenant farmers are now buying their land from the landlords with money loaned at good rates through the British Parliament. My brother Séamus will own the land we have worked for generations. That is good."

Johnny was dismissive.

"Nothing but full freedom is enough!"

Cahal would agree with that. It was time to visit one of Fitzgerald beer halls at day's end.

Later Cahal told Johnny that he wanted to make contact with the Hennessys and meet his daughter. As he used the word he knew that he spoke without doubt and the word 'daughter' reverberated and repeated and thrilled. He wanted to whisper, speak, shout, roar again and again 'daughter

daughter daughter'. No doubt! He had never doubted and if he had it was an attempt to counter persistent heartbreak.
"Be careful, Cahal," Johnny advised
"I know and I worry and I have refrained from searching with great difficulty, but while I was at home in Lough Gur I knew that the time had come when I could no longer postpone. I knew I had to find Con and Mary and my daughter."
Johnny put his hands on his shoulders, held briefly and then slapped him on the back.
"A good politician has no difficulty finding people. People are votes!"
They laughed. It was the end of a wonderful day.

The next morning they went together to Keany's office. Finding the whereabouts of Con and Mary Hennessy in New York was a priority on that day. By evening Cahal knew where they lived, where he had to go. It was time for farewells and a return to New York.

"So you've been back home," Con said wistfully.
Cahal was sitting in the kitchen of Hennessy's apartment in the Bronx. Even though they were happy to see him Con and Mary had some reservations in regard to Kate. They had much to talk about. It had been over twenty years since their short encounter on board ship. Two relationships had formed on that voyage. Con and Mary were still together, still in love, industrious and prospering in the New World. Cahal and Kate did not get the same chance. Death took Kate away and Cahal was left with a terrible lost love. Soon he would see young Kate, his own daughter.
"Lots of changes at home, Con, many of them for the good. The biggest change was in my mother. I will not see her again in this life. Nor my father either for that matter. I don't know if I will ever see home again."

Mary and Con hung on his words and asked him a thousand questions, and the 'music' of Galtee Mountains, Lake of Lough Gur, Galbally, Knockainey and rivers and streams and bogs and hills filled that little room. As the evening settled in they waited for Kate's return home from the hospital where she worked as a nurse. They spoke of their voyage and Cahal asked about the fiddler from Barraduff as they recalled the night of the storm.

"Ah, Dan Murphy! Still delighting everybody with his music. He now owns a tavern and it's the best place in the Bronx for the Irish music. We will visit him tonight. Indeed he has often asked about you, Cahal."

Back to Ireland!

"Are we any nearer to freedom, Cahal?"
"Not the full freedom we seek, Con, but there is talk of Home Rule, which would give limited freedom and who knows what might follow."
"The Rebellion of '98 and poor Robert Emmet's effort will be commemorated in the coming years. Then the young men will reach for the guns again."
"Too much fighting and killing we've had. May God protect them!" was Mary's comment.

Kate had lived as daughter to Con and Mary, and their five children were her brothers and sisters. However, she knew that her mother had died giving her birth, and Mary had told her of a great brief love between her mother and a young man on board the ship. His name was not mentioned and Kate chose to put this knowledge deep down in the recesses of her mind, to forget as far as possible. When Cahal had made contact with Con and Mary they had insisted that as far as Kate was concerned he was a friend coming to visit.

Whether or not he would disclose paternity to Kate was something to be decided later. As far as Con was concerned Cahal was Kate's father. He did not know, was never told by his dead sister that the landlord's son had savagely molested her. Whatever anger he may have felt at Kate's pregnancy and death had dissipated in his love for his niece.

The door opened and Kate entered. For Cahal time stopped and went into reverse. There stood the girl who spoke words of love so many years ago. She had remained young and beautiful. His pulse raced, words of love screamed within his head. The words of introduction he vaguely heard and her hand was in his. The first meeting of father and daughter is not without recognition; some primal instinct stirs; a moment so momentous impacts; emotions explode; sanity is retained with difficulty for the knowing one. If Cahal had ever doubted it was now no more. Wonderful lovely lost Kate, but the eyes holding his were his mother's young eyes Exultation, heartbreak, unconfined joy, sadness, to have found his daughter but not allowed to acknowledge. He wanted to hold her, love her, but their hands parted and reality returned.
"I am pleased to meet you, Mr. Hayes," as she semi-curtsied.
Con said, "We met Mr. Hayes coming over on the ship…" and stopped abruptly as Kate's knowing glance told him that he had divulged the secret. She turned to the man who had come to visit.
"Are you my father, Mr. Hayes?"
"Yes!" and his heart was bursting with pride and love and joy.

EPILOGUE.

Lost love accelerated into being the reality it should always have been. Kate, the nurse, grew to love her father in a short period of days. Cahal had found a young ear eager to listen and he had many things to tell her. He told her about her mother and their brief love together, of life in Ireland and San Francisco, of her grandparents and cousins in Lough Gur. She was particularly fascinated when he told her the story of the Sun Shield. They walked for hours in the park and Cahal felt the elation of release. This 'young' Kate gave him solace and understanding and a seed of love followed on the seed that gave life. Their relationship grew into a most marvellous father-daughter bond. And all of this happened within the ten days of his New York stopover

Kate was engaged to marry Michael Crimmins, young emigrant from Glin in Co. Limerick, a skilled mason who could earn a good living. With help from Cahal, Michael was able to set up his own construction company. None prouder than Cahal when he linked his daughter to the high altar in St. Patrick's in the Bronx on Shrove Tuesday 1897 and gave her to Michael to be his bride. The previous Friday he had been in St. Stephen's in Boston as godfather to John Francis Junior, fourth child of John Francis and Mary Josephine Fitzgerald. The following year he was in New York to be godfather to baby Michael Crimmins, named after his late paternal grandfather. Their second son would be called Cahal. In all there were four children in the family when they moved to San Francisco in 1902. Opportunity for Cahal to leave the Kenneally house without selling it. Michael, Kate and family settled in. Cahal bought a penthouse apartment on Grant Avenue. He would never marry. He didn't need to. He had family.

In a way Nefa Rua salved her guilt in the convent in Clonmacnoise. Had she returned to Aney then her facial deformity would not have prevented her marriage to Garvok. When she finally returned irreparable damage had been done. She shunned company other than her house-slave, refused to meet Garvok, gave birth to a child, which she killed immediately after birth. She then sent messengers to tribes near and far offering big rewards to young warriors who would come and fight for her. When she had adequate complement she attacked Carraig Aille, obsessed with the idea that Garvok was the cause of all her troubles. She was convinced that only in his death and her getting the Sun Shield could she be salved again.

On January 1st 1906 the Honorable John Francis Fitzgerald was inducted as Mayor of Boston. Cahal was there to celebrate his victory. They had remained steadfast friends and regularly visited each other. Another baby born to Kate and Michael in San Francisco and now they had four boys and three girls. Cahal was happy in himself and for them. On the night of April 19th of that year a tumultuous earthquake shattered San Francisco. Cahal's high-rise apartment was an immediate victim. As the building collapsed Cahal's life ended. In his final fleeting moments images flashed through his mind of Sun Shield and Séamus, of Mary and Kate, of young Kate and his grandchildren. Lough Gur was calling to him but darkness enveloped and he could not answer the call.

She would not have the Sun Shield. He had given it to the lake gods. Much weakened from his wounds he was now alone, the last defender of Carraig Aille. He did not understand why Nefa Rua wanted to kill him. The gates shattered and he heard the shouts of victory. It was over! He saw her among the warriors and had a fleeting moment of hope. He stood transfixed. The charge! The cast of the spear! He felt it enter his chest. The shouting was frozen in Nefa Rua's despairing cry. She ran to him and cradled his head to her breast, rocking to and fro in awful sorrow!

***The End*.**